You can do this, she told herself. *You've done it literally hundreds of times. Chances are, all you'll need to do is put a scare in them, anyway.*

She realized that her palms were clenched tightly and that she was sweating profusely. *Thank you, fear.*

She forced herself to work it out: all she had to do, she knew, was take out the big dude. Once he was overpowered, his sad little cronies would surely fall into line. And since they had their backs to her and were infinitely consumed with their work, she had the element of surprise working in her favor, in addition to her years of training. She willed her trembling limbs to steady and thought back to this afternoon, how she'd been able to break up the mugging with relatively little difficulty. It didn't matter that she was terror girl these days. Frightened or not, she still had to bust a little ass kicking.

Don't miss any books in this thrilling series:

FEARLESS™

Available from SIMON PULSE

FEARLESS™

WIRED

FRANCINE PASCAL

SIMON PULSE
New York London Toronto Sydney

First Simon Pulse edition May 2004

Copyright © 2004 by Francine Pascal

Cover copyright © 2004 by 17th Street Productions, an Alloy company.

SIMON PULSE
An imprint of Simon & Schuster Children's Publishing Division
1230 Avenue of the Americas, New York, NY 10020

 Produced by 17th Street Productions,
an Alloy company
151 West 26th Street
New York, NY 10001

Fearless™ is a trademark of Francine Pascal.

Printed in the United States of America
10 9 8 7 6 5 4 3 2 1

Library of Congress Control Number: 2004100271
ISBN: 0-689-86916-9

To Kelty O'Brien

God garden-
wasn't
interested. variety
He had freaks
other
things on and
his weirdos
mind.

WASHINGTON SQUARE PARK WASN'T

really the place to be at twilight. Not by a long shot.

Emulation of Innocence

In the daytime it was pleasant enough. Bright, sunny, and manageable in size, the park was generally populated by a fresh cross section of skate punks, middle-aged hippies, NYU students, would-be actresses walking their dogs, and older folk drinking coffee by the fountain that lay squarely at the park's midpoint.

But even the brightest blaze of sunshine, the most unmarred of blue skies couldn't fully hide the way the idyllic scene tended to unravel at the edges. Burnt-out stoner types leered from against lush trees, on the lookout to score a deal for pot or sometimes coke or even harder stuff. Homeless people camped on benches, deterring locals from perching for any extended period. The less savory the activity, the more likely one was to find it at night. Once the sun receded, the cover of darkness provided shadow enough for the criminal element, rendering the park less than safe for anyone unschooled in the art of self-protection. And though many New Yorkers operated under a false sense of security, a notion that they could take care of themselves, they were, by and large, wrong. All the martial arts classes in the world weren't really going to do a person much good against a man with a gun.

Case in point: In a far corner of the park, to the right of the miniature Arc de Triomphe and just beyond the now-abandoned dog run, a young girl struggled against a band of male hoods. They had the upper hand, but she was slipping through their fingers. It was obvious even to the casual observer that she was a trained fighter. Whatever they were trying to do to her—and it was unclear, from this distance—she was going to escape. Even if only by a hair.

It was no matter. God wasn't interested. He had other things on his mind.

God had arrived in the park earlier to give the people what they wanted. To pass along his magic so that human beings could fulfill their fantasies of being invincible. Though if the hoods in the distance were any indication, some dreams were an inch or two shy of being attainable. Invincibility was beyond some people's reach. But hope springs eternal.

And God could bring them closer. His medicine could bring them closer to invincibility, immortality. And for the right price, he was happy to help.

A scuffle against the pavement told him that

3

someone was coming up the walkway. He turned to see two uniformed policemen, the taller of the two swinging a flashlight down the asphalt path. God rearranged his features in an emulation of inno- cence as the flashlight's beam cut across his face.

"Hello," he called. It was almost a question. As if to imply that should the police be looking toward him for any relevant information, they'd be barking up the wrong tree. He squinted plaintively, stuffing his hands into the pockets of his long gray coat.

"Have you seen anything unusual around here?" Taller called out, somewhat out of breath. "Tonight, that is?"

"Not really. I just got here," God protested. "Was out for a quick walk and a smoke." He held up his cig- arette out of his pocket by way of demonstration.

The policemen no longer seemed suspicious of him, only curious. "So, do you, uh, walk in the park often?" Tall wanted to know. "Can't be so safe."

"Most nights. It helps clear my head."

"Have you seen any suspicious characters lately?"

"Are you looking for someone specific? Maybe if you described him or her?" God asked.

"That's just it," the smaller one chimed in. "We don't know exactly what he looks like. But there's a new player in the park, goes by the name of God. We think he's been peddling a new drug called Invince. Makes people feel invincible, like. Hasn't been approved by any drug company, of course. . . and it isn't going to be any-time soon. Dangerous stuff."

"Is it like Ecstasy?" God wanted to know.

"Worse. It has a lot of the same effects on the body—drains it of anything good, that is—but it riles people up. Makes them very aggressive." It was obvious that the officers were aiming for intimida-tion. Little did they have any clue who they were dealing with.

God shrugged. "I'm sorry, but I really haven't seen anything. You know, nothing worse than your garden-variety freaks and weirdos."

Taller clapped him on the back. "That's all right, son. But consider yourself warned: Invince is bad news, and so are the people who are on it. You see any-thing, anything at all unusual going on around here, you avoid it. You get the hell out of the park. Better yet, you come down to the station and tell one of us about it. So far, all we've heard are rumors. If we want to stop the wave of violence, we're gonna have to get to the source. The person who's selling. This God guy. Assuming he exists—drug addicts aren't always the most reliable witnesses. Anyway, you come to us."

God nodded. "I sure will, Officers. You know, if I see anything."

God stubbed out his cigarette with the heel of his boot, turned, and stalked off into the night, deeper into the cover of the park.

There's a reason that a cliché becomes a cliché, right? I mean, these phrases aren't chosen as part of everyone's daily rotation based on one loser's decision. It's because people, day in and day out, find truth in these expressions.

Beauty is in the eye of the beholder. Yeah, I know that one. For instance, when I look in the mirror, I see a hulking freak show of a girl with gangly muscles and a total lack of fashion sense. But given that Ed, Sam, and Jake—three empirically hot guys in their own right—seem to find me reasonably attractive, I can assume that maybe—just maybe—they see something when they look at me that I can't see in myself. Some kernel of normal girlness. Something girlfriendworthy. And the fact that any of them showed the slightest bit of faith in my ability to be like other girls makes me believe that the possibility exists.

Curiosity killed the cat. So I

heard about the possibility of
gene therapy, and I thought, *Why
not?* After all, being born without a fear gene is one of the
primary causes of my social inep-
titude: I am fearless, ergo, I am
utterly unfeminine and unable to
relate to my peers. So logic
would dictate that by introducing
a fear gene into my system
through the wonders of science,
I'd bring myself one step closer
to understanding the typical ado-
lescent experience.

Normal is as normal does. Who
was I kidding? "Normal" is more
than just the absence or presence
of fear. Normal is for girls who
have a traditional nuclear family
instead of a mother who was killed
by her father's evil twin and an
MIA secret agent man for a father.
Girls who don't have to worry that
any of their friends will be tar-
geted by dangerous forces, hunted
down, and possibly killed.
"Normal" girls don't wander into
Washington Square Park at night,
looking to pick a fight. Girl

power is all well and good, but
normal girls have a sense of self-
preservation that I, even with my
brand-spanking-new fear gene, seem
to lack. Other people take their
cues from fear, but since I am so
new to this full range of human
emotions, I am crippled by my own.
Like a moron, I went after a thug,
and like a victim, I was attacked.
Like a normal girl, I am tearing
down the street, fleeing from the
scene. . . terrified. And though
my reaction is entirely normal, I
know in my heart that a *truly* normal girl wouldn't have gone to the
park at all. In the delicate
karmic balance of my own biochemistry, the acquisition of a fear
gene must be canceled out through
the immediate removal of the common sense gene. Who cares if, with
all of my GI training, I could
have taken those guys out? *I
shouldn't have tried.* It's scary,
and it's that simple.

I should have known, though.
It's like that old cliché goes:
Be careful what you wish for.

I can hardly be surprised that I've estranged myself from anyone I might wish to be close with: friends and family have all lost interest in showing me their trust again, and I cannot blame them. As Loki, I visited all forms of evil upon them without any sense of remorse or regret, and people will not simply bounce back from that. I've thought long and hard about those to whom I wish to make amends, those to whom I'll apologize despite the inadequacy of the phrase. I've made a literal list, and I've begun to make my way through it.

But at the top, the bottom, and throughout is Gaia.

Gaia Moore, my beautiful, eminently strong niece—she who, under a different set of circumstances, could have been my own daughter, does not trust me. There is no rectifying that, and without her forgiveness, any other name on the list is meaningless.

I have done what I can to show

my sincerity to her. I organized
a rescue mission when her father,
my twin, needed me; I have
attempted to make amends with Sam
Moon and to foster a relationship
with Gaia's boyfriend, Jake
Montone. But ultimately all that
I do, I do for her.

She is in danger, this I know.
I haven't yet uncovered who is
after her, but I will. And while
Gaia typically does not need protection, fearless and trained as
she is, I will keep close watch
over her until the danger has
passed.

And it's fortunate, indeed,
that I persist in my attempts to
protect her despite her lack of
interest in me: though Gaia is
typically endlessly brave, just
tonight I may have saved her
life. I pulled her from those
boys in the street and saved her
from a beating and God knows what
else. I, Uncle Oliver—not Loki.

Yet Gaia ran from me, contin-
ues to run from me. She is not
interested in my reparations or

my warnings. Saving her life is not proof enough of my intentions.

No matter. If she won't listen to reason, I'll merely redouble my efforts. Dig deeper, reconnect with old contacts. Follow her more closely. I am Oliver these days, yet I find the fight against my Loki urges increasingly more difficult. And though I can't succumb to his urges or malevolent fantasies, I can say this with assurance: His instincts are never wrong.

Gaia is in danger. I can feel it. I will stop it. At any cost.

GAIA POUNDED DOWN THE STREET

That Fight-or-Flight Thing

blindly, sprinting toward Jake's apartment at breakneck speed. She was still recovering from the fight she'd just had in front of her apartment. She'd gotten into a cab after the Rodke party, and some thugs had been waiting to pounce on her when she'd pulled up in front of her apartment.

They were hopped up on false confidence—also known as Invince. Unfortunately, she was hopped up on fear generated by a recent procedure she'd had done. She'd wanted to be fearless so that she could experience life just like other people did. She assumed that, trained as she was in all mainstream forms of martial arts, fear could be channeled into an asset: adrenaline would fuel her power, and that fight-or-flight thing would kick in, and she'd be on fire. She was all about *fight*.

It was *flight* Gaia hadn't counted on.

Other people, she supposed, relied on fear as a means of self-preservation, a way of motivating themselves out of danger. But those guys hadn't been much danger. Hell, they were hardly more than boys—she'd taken larger groups, bigger men, with scarier weapons, on plenty of other occasions.

It was the fear.

She just hadn't acclimated herself to it yet. That last fight she'd had with Jake—when she'd run—hadn't made it easier for her to calibrate her response. But the adrenaline surge that normally came during a fight, propelling her into graceful but deadly—and, most importantly, clearheaded—motion had been replaced by sheer, chaotic panic. That, more than any logical thought, had incited Gaia to get the hell out of there before things could go from bad to worse.

Her heart still raced. She shuddered, as much from embarrassment as from lingering terror. *Get a grip, Gaia*, she told herself. Sure, Jake could be of comfort, but did she really want him to see her like this? This might be a little *too* much like other girls, looking to boyfriends for reassurance. But she couldn't help it. If there was a balance between vulnerability and inner strength, she hadn't found it yet.

Arriving at Jake's place, she smoothed an errant strand of hair off her sweaty forehead in a lame attempt to pull herself together. She straightened her wrinkled black dress as best she could. The effort was useless, she knew. The elevator door slid open and she marched toward his door. In a fun new twist, the general, vague uncertainty she usually felt when confronted with any typical boyfriend-girlfriend situation seemed to have been replaced with a more acute form of pre-Jake anxiety.

13

Perfect. Just what I need after a near-death experience. More anxiety.

As soon as that thought left her brain, Jake's door swung open. He stood in front of her, clearly surprised. "Gaia?" he said, puzzled, hiking up his jeans and tugging quickly at his mussed black T-shirt to smooth it out. He moved back to allow her entrance. "What's up?" he asked, ushering her into his bedroom. Clearly he hadn't been expecting company. "Are you okay?" He stepped closer, taking a look at her disheveled appearance.

Gaia swallowed. "I, uh, was near the boarding-house. You know. And it was late. And there were these guys. . . ." She trailed off. She heard how she sounded, heard the neediness in her own voice, and she was completely put off by it. She didn't want to tell Jake how frightened she'd been.

She didn't have to say the words. Jake took her hand. "Gaia, did they attack you? Did they hurt you? Jeez, what were you thinking? I know you're, like, superhero strong, but did you ever think that maybe you should give it a rest for a while? I mean, starting up with dangerous people? Come on."

Gaia surprised them both by bursting into a sudden fit of tears that subsided as quickly as they began. "I know," she gasped, wiping angrily at her eyes. "Don't think I don't know."

Jake folded her into his arms gently, his words taking

a more soothing tone. "I didn't mean to come off like a jerk—I just worry about you. I know you can take care of yourself, but still. . . it's a new experience for me, dating Lara Croft." He smiled teasingly at her and kissed her on her forehead, running his hands over her back soothingly.

She managed a small grin. "I'm learning about the fine line between taking care of oneself and looking for trouble," she agreed. "Tonight was definitely looking."

"I'm just glad you're not hurt." Jake shuddered, as if envisioning the attack. "So how did you get away?"

Gaia's features darkened, and she trembled again. "It was Lo—I mean, it was Oliver, I guess. He just appeared out of nowhere and scared the creeps off. He had a gun." A troubled glance crossed her face. "He's still following me. I can't believe he's totally ignoring the fact that I asked him to stop."

"Wait a minute," Jake cut in, taking in her wary expression. "So you're being held at knifepoint, and your uncle comes up and pretty much saves your life—and you're angry? Gaia, I know you've been on edge lately—certainly getting shaken up more easily than I'm used to—but come on. Can't you cut him some slack? I mean, based on what you're telling me, it sounds like you could have been seriously hurt if he hadn't shown up when he did, right? I hope you didn't give him a hard time."

Gaia looked away for a moment. "I ran away," she said curtly, without meeting Jake's gaze. She couldn't look him in the eye.

"You ran away? For chrissake, *why*?"

She heard the annoyance in his tone—it would have been pretty impossible to miss—and felt a brief flicker of anger herself. "Listen, you weren't there, okay?" she said. "I sort of freaked, I know. But. . . I have to tell you, I don't trust him." She could tell that the edge in her voice wasn't winning her any points with Jake.

"I know you don't trust him, Gaia. We all know you don't trust him," Jake said sarcastically. "And I know there are gaps in my understanding of your history with him. But I gotta tell you, until you fill me in on the whole do, I'm going to continue thinking that you're taking this old grudge too far."

"And I have to tell *you* that you don't know anything about it, Jake," Gaia argued, her voice rising. "I know you think that just because we went on one rescue mission together, you understand the whole cloak-and-dagger aspect of my life, but believe me when I say that was just the tip of the iceberg." She softened her tone, hoping to convince him through the sheer weight of her emotion. "It's true, he's apologized over and over again and gone out of his way to win back my loyalty. And that has to count for something. It *does* count for something," she corrected herself. "That's why I forgave him, why I was willing to give him a second chance.

"But you don't know him like I do. And when Oliver starts acting suspiciously, well... you have to be suspicious. Oliver helped to save my father, sure, but he can't really take back the things he's done over the years or make up for them. And even when I'm trying to rebuild my trust for him, it's hard to take him back into my life, no questions asked. I can't just let my guard down completely. Too much has happened. And frankly, when I feel like a member of my own family is *stalking* me, I can't help but be concerned." Her anger was mounting. "If you knew the things that I know, Jake, you'd get it. Because it's not just my own safety at stake. When Oliver gets close to me. . . he hurts the people I care about."

And that includes you, okay? she thought. *He killed my mother, he hurt my father, he kidnapped Sam, and he went after Ed. You do the math. I know I forgave him, but if there's even the remotest chance that he's defected back to the dark side, then I'm going to have to be on the offensive. I'm not prepared to fall for his lies again just to watch him add you to the list of casualties.* Until she was ready to give Jake the full story, though, she'd have to keep that to herself. Which meant she'd have to risk allowing him to think she was overreacting.

Jake's features were set in a stony mask of disapproval,

a scowling gargoyle glaring down at her. His arms were folded unrelentingly across his chest. It was clear that the gravity of her warnings was eluding him. Fighting alongside Oliver had obviously made Jake feel like the last action hero and had engendered a misguided sense of loyalty.

Great. Not only was her boyfriend not going to console her, but he was pretty much defecting to the enemy's camp. Simply put, Jake wasn't seeing Gaia's viewpoint at all. This fear thing was proving to be fun for the whole family.

Gaia sighed and turned to go. She hated leaving things unresolved, but really—what more was there to say?

"I'm sorry, Jake, that you don't understand how I feel about my uncle. But to be honest, I hope you never get to the point where you do." She kissed him quickly on the cheek and quietly showed herself the door.

GAIA FUMED AS SHE LOPED UP THE stairs of the Christopher Street station two steps at a time. The regular, normal-girl part **Suckiness** of her that liked having a boyfriend and *seriously* liked Jake hated the conversation that they'd just had and couldn't stand that they hadn't been able to talk things out. But the other Gaia, the Gaia who had lived fearlessly through seventeen years, understood that suckiness was her destiny. The stars were obviously aligned against her, and no amount of genetic mutation would change that. With all this fear coursing through her veins, she was entirely unstable but still incapable of doing whatever it was that other teenage girls did. It would have been funny if it weren't so pathetic.

Still, she had allowed herself the slightest bit of hope that Jake would give her the benefit of the doubt, that he'd acknowledge that when it came to Oliver, at least, Gaia had the goods, that perhaps her judgment was to be trusted. He was her boyfriend, right? He was supposed to be on her side. Wasn't he?

Thoughts this dour required an immediate sugar fix. Ice cream was the key, Gaia decided. She paused on Seventh Avenue and darted into the Häagen-Dazs, a blast of cold air greeting her as she ducked in. Surveying the dazzling array of flavors, she wasted no time in ordering a single-scoop cone of chocolate-chocolate chip.

"Two thirty-nine," the sour-faced attendant barked at her from underneath his brown-striped visor, not bothering with even a glance in her direction. He'd been deeply engaged in conversation with an acne-scarred stock boy and clearly resented the interruption. He rang up Gaia's purchase and dropped her change into her palm with a scowl. Unfazed, Gaia ignored his total lack of manners and dove in, shoving the door open with her hip. A surly cashier was no reason to waste a perfectly good ice-cream cone.

Striding back in the direction of the boarding-house and struggling to avoid an ice-cream headache, Gaia turned her thoughts back to Sam. He had been the one to first notice that Oliver might be reverting to his evil alter ego, Loki, and he had immediately come to warn Gaia. She flushed with the memory. At the time she had been concerned that Sam was looking for excuses to talk to her, maybe trying to rekindle their romance. Sure, he had told her that he needed to move on, to get her out of his life, and she didn't blame him—she was sure that every time he looked at her, he must be reminded of his horrifying kidnapping—but then he kept turning up. And no matter how she felt about Jake, it was impossible to deny her lingering connection with Sam. After all, they shared the type of history most people never knew.

Of course, maybe he *was* legitimately worried. He, of course, would know better than anyone what Loki was capable of when he was carrying out a vendetta. One thing she was certain of now: Sam knew how Gaia felt about her uncle, and he'd never prey on her fears in a sleazy attempt to reconnect with her. If he was worried, there was probably good reason for it.

She fished her cell phone out of her pocket and called up her phone book. Sam's new number was the third entry. She scrolled through her negligible directory until his name appeared on the screen. Her fingers hovered over the call button, hesitating.

Gaia was so frustrated. Why would her own boyfriend refuse to see her side of things? Why couldn't he just take her word for it? Was Sam truly the only person who understood Gaia intrinsically? Was she fated to live mired in the past, unable to bond with someone who hadn't lived through the horrors of her life with her? Did this mean that Jake would never understand her? That she could never move on?

It figured.

She stopped in front of a newspaper dispenser, seeing that the latest free *Village Voice* had been distributed. She could use a little left-wing polemic to lighten the load of the day she'd had. Whatever. She'd go back to the boardinghouse, crash, maybe read some hipper-than-thou movie reviews, and put this whole encounter out of her mind. She leaned forward and reached into the dispenser, grabbing a paper from the top of the stack, slamming the door shut, and straightening again.

Wham! "Hi, pretty girl," a face murmured, hovering without warning mere inches from her own, dry lips stretching across yellowed teeth. "Can I have one, too?"

It was a random homeless man—totally common for New York City and especially common on a random Village street corner. She knew, without looking, that the streets weren't completely deserted, that there were any number of corner markets where she could quickly seek solace if she were truly concerned. But this man was no threat. Possibly lacking a screw or two, *definitely* in desperate need of a toothbrush, but not dangerous. She *knew* all of this reflexively.

It didn't matter. She jumped, shrank back from his probing hands, and without a word turned and fled.

Though she tried her best to keep her pace even, she retreated pretty damn quickly. She practically ran.

She practically ran like a *girl.*

From: gaia13@alloymail.com
To: smoon@alloymail.com
Re: Oliver

Sam—

I know we talked about your needing to start a new life, on your own, and I don't blame you for needing some distance from me. When I think about the dangers I involved you in, I don't have the words to apologize. So I will let you move on, but I need to tell you one thing: I think you were right. About Oliver, that is. I think he's. . . losing control. I think Loki is coming back. And I don't know what to do. I don't know what I'll do if—

[delete]

From: gaia13@alloymail.com
To: shred@alloymail.com
Re: Fear

Ed—

I won't even bother to pretend that I didn't just freak out in the hospital with you. There'd be no point, since for some strange and totally irritating reason you always seem to be able to see right through me. And since you can read me anyway, I figure I might as well tell you what was going on with me in that room. What's been going on with me, how I may have made a huge mistake, and now suddenly I am fearful of every creak on the staircase—

[delete]

Jake was obviously
more partial
to a contrite and

questionable

touchy- **genetic**
feely
Gaia **mutation**

than to a stubborn,
hard-ass Gaia.

"YOU ARE GOING TO LOVE ME," KAI proclaimed, taking a bright pink vinyl messenger bag off her shoulder, setting it down on one of the uncomfortable molded plastic chairs reserved for hospital visitors, and producing from

Internal Monologue

within it a `monster-sized chocolate chip cookie`. She leaned across the bed and handed it to Ed. "Courtesy of Taylor's. Since I know the hospital food was starting to get you down," she explained. "And we have to keep your strength up."

"Excellent. But what will *you* eat?" Ed teased. The cookie was easily big enough to feed three people. He broke off a hunk and chewed blissfully.

"This may be your last chance for rebellion against the hospital diet," Kai mused aloud. "Seeing as how you're going to be sprung tomorrow." She seemed as thrilled about it as Ed was, if that were possible.

"We should enjoy this while it lasts," Ed agreed. "You rock. You're like a `crazed escape artist` or something, ditching school and smuggling contraband junk food into the hospital. I'm leading you into a life of crime. I'm bringing you down."

"I'll be Bonnie to your Clyde, no problem. I live for danger," Kai assured him.

Ed grinned through a mouthful of chocolate. With

her graphic T-shirt and oversized lavender cords, Kai didn't look particularly dangerous, but he was willing to play along. After all, he was genuinely glad that although they'd agreed not to date, he and Kai really could be friends. He still felt a little bit guilty that he hadn't been able to be a true boyfriend to her. Apparently he was so lame that he was still sort of semi-pining over Gaia, but shockingly, Kai had been totally understanding, and their breakup had been refreshingly drama free. One more reason why he was a total freak not to be with her. But it was okay. He was just glad that they could still enjoy each other's company. Jokes about killer couples on the lam had much more to do with her low-key attitude than with any lingering feelings for him, he was sure. He nudged a piece of cookie at Kai, but she refused it.

"I just ate," she protested. "Anyway, it's for you."

Ed frowned. He couldn't get used to Kai's birdlike appetite. Sure, he had dated Heather Gannis, and she and her cronies had practically been *born* on the South Beach Diet, but lately he'd been spoiled by women with heartier appetites.

Woman, Fargo. One woman.

He tried to push the thought out of his mind, but it was true. There was one woman he knew with the ability to outeat a trucker, and despite the fact that Kai was beaming amicably at him with electric-blue-rimmed eyes, he couldn't get that one woman out of his mind.

Gaia.

Was he destined to live out his days like this, impossibly hooked on a girl he couldn't have? He and Gaia had been friends—*best* friends—and then more than friends, and here they were, things more awkward than ever. She'd gotten back together with her ex, Sam, or so Ed had thought (she swore they weren't involved, but it didn't take a genius to read the way they looked at each other), and now she was clearly being courted by Jake Montone. And she didn't seem to mind one bit.

Ed wished he could believe that the only reason Gaia was on his mind was because she had been acting so strange lately. The last time she visited him, she was skittish, practically afraid of her own shadow—not at all the kick-ass chick he'd fallen in love with. And she had seriously wigged when he mentioned Heather's visit from the CIA. So much so that he'd refrained from ever following up with her, which was a `direct violation of their no-BS policy`. He himself wasn't convinced that ignoring what had happened with Heather was a good idea, but he didn't think now was the time to dig deeper with Gaia—and he didn't know who else to turn to.

So yeah, it made perfect sense for Ed to be thinking about Gaia in the context of a concerned friend, to be sure. He'd have to be a coldhearted freak not to notice when his ex–best friend/girlfriend/who the hell knew what suddenly went from being crouching tiger to being afraid of her own shadow. But as for what to do about it, he had no idea whatsoever.

"Ed, your call," Kai admonished, her voice breaking into his reverie.

"Huh? What?" It took Ed a minute to recover from his little `internal monologue`. *Smooth, Fargo,* he told himself as he frantically swept cookie crumbs from the bedspread to the floor. "Here. All clean."

"Right, 'cause I'm such a neat freak," she said, smiling. "Forgot the crumbs. Obviously you were totally captivated by what I was just saying. Listen: big-decision time. Daytime television gives us two choices: you've got soaps or talk shows. Your call."

And that was just it. Plain and simple. Kai always made the choices easy for him. But it didn't make him feel any more for her. It didn't make her. . . Gaia.

From: tammiejammie@alloymail.com
To: megan21@alloymail.com
Re: Prom attire

So—

   Just saw the cutest dress *ever* at BCBG SoHo during lunch. I put it on hold. Wanna come after school to check it out? Would *love* a second opinion.

From: megan21@alloymail.com
To: tammiejammie@alloymail.com
Re: Re: Prom attire

Totally. Can't wait. But don't you think it'll be hard to, like, totally get into the spirit of prom and graduation and stuff with all of the serious stuff going on lately? I mean, Ed in the hospital and that creepy "Droog" violence? It freaks me out.

And speaking of creepy, just saw Gaia Moore in her usual sweats du jour—big change from the little black dress of Wednesday night, you know? I mean, could someone please get the girl a brush? Tell me what a hottie like Jake Montone—who *clearly* understands the importance of personal grooming—sees in a girl like that? I'm still thinking we should plan a little low-level revenge since she did lie to us about the party—whether everyone else is into it or not.

Anyway, let's meet on the steps after last period. I need caffeine if I'm going to keep my strength up shopping.

LOCAL DROOGS ENGAGE IN A LITTLE
OF THE OLD ULTRAVIOLENCE

IV heads, or "Droogs," as they are coming to be known by the media, may have a new way of getting their fix. The next wave of testosterone highs comes from an "Orange," so named because it comes in the form of a tab stamped with small orange polka-dot icons. These "Oranges" are the most concentrated form of IV available, and those who're hooked are acting out *Clockwork Orange* style—that is to say, indulging in a little of the old ultraviolence. IV almost completely inhibits fear, leaving those who've taken it free to wreak havoc around town in the form of pranks—some harmless, some less so. Police report that vandalism is up 12 percent since Oranges hit the scene and petty burglary 22 percent. Washington Square Park, sources report, has been heavily hit, and it is recommended that Village School students avoid the park after sundown.

"You don't want to be out in the park—or even anywhere near there—once the sun is down," Sergeant Mike Donovan warns. "The Droogs aren't like other JDs. They're more like serious addicts. Which means dangerous with a capital *D*. They're not afraid of anything."

With prom and graduation rapidly approaching, we at the Village School have to wonder if the escalation of IV-related crimes is going to rain on our end-of-the-year parade. Prom night, for example, traditionally known for its high levels of underage drinking and drug use, may be more closely monitored. But according to Principal Hickey, there are at present no intentions to alter plans for graduation or prom. "We see no reason not to carry on as usual," Hickey confirmed, "though we may heighten our security. Neither graduation nor prom should be affected by this recent wave of petty crime."

Which means that for the time being, at least, prom and graduation—as well as all related events and ceremonies—will continue as planned.

GAIA FINISHED SKIMMING THE NEWS-
paper article in the latest
Village School Weekly and
pushed the paper aside. She
picked listlessly at her lunch—
something vaguely Italian swam
in a sea of watery red sauce, but
it wasn't doing the trick—and
thought about the Droogs. So
they were fearless, huh? It was
ironic that this group of tweak-

Sudden Burst of Optimism

ers would replicate her very own questionable
genetic mutation at the same time that she was
acutely, unavoidably fearing just about everything
that she encountered. The idea of a bunch of scum-
bags getting their jollies in *her* park, making life
unsafe for *her* friends was the type of thing that
would normally have motivated her to kick some
serious ass. She'd have *deliberately* headed to the park,
looking for losers to stomp on. But now? Now she
found herself distractedly thinking about prom,
relieved, surprisingly, to hear that it was going to be
held as usual but uncertain as to whether or not she'd
be in attendance.

"You finished with that?" A skate rat she recognized as one of Ed's pre-accident thrill seekers leaned
over her shoulder to get a better glimpse of the newspaper headline. He was breathing all over her Italian

surprise, she noted, which did nothing to enhance her interest in it.

"Huh? Yeah, take it." Gaia practically shoved the paper at him to get him off her back and out of her personal space. She pushed her lunch tray farther away, certain she wasn't going to touch it again.

"Sucks about prom, right?" the skate rat continued, smiling affably enough at her. Incredibly, he didn't seem to be picking up on her leave-me-alone vibe.

She managed a halfhearted grin. She definitely couldn't afford to alienate any other member of the student body, especially right now, after she'd pretty much killed any real chance she had of fitting in with the FOHs. Her internal monitors were on the fritz. Everyone was putting her on edge, and even the most benign gesture set off her sensors. Gaia wasn't exactly warm and fuzzy under the best of circumstances, but this was extreme. "I guess," she grunted.

"Maybe we'll still get to have it like normal," he responded, clearly inspired by a sudden burst of optimism. He gestured toward the paper one last time and, convinced Gaia didn't mind parting with it, tucked it under his arm and loped away.

"Right, like normal," Gaia muttered to herself.

A few months ago Gaia wouldn't have even dreamed of going to the prom. Prom was for girls like Megan and Tammie and the other FOHs, girls who knew about things like using "products" and about the benefits of eyelash curlers. Gaia's idea of getting ready for school was to fish out her least wrinkled sweatshirt from the pile on her floor.

But something had happened to Gaia slowly, steadily, in the time she'd been at the Village School. No, she hadn't impressed her teachers with her photographic memory—she was absent too often for anyone to be blown away by her intellect—but she *had* managed to somehow end her seventeen-year stint as Gaia the Unkissed and venture into the territory of Gaia the Girlfriend. Oh, sure, two of her three love interests had either been kidnapped or otherwise tortured by her uncle and the various other evil forces acting on her life, and the third had just tagged along for a search-and-rescue mission to *Siberia*, but why quibble?

No, the point was that somehow, Gaia was slowly learning to fit in. She'd made a handful of friends and even gone to a party or two. And the new girl in school, Liz Rodke, seemed distinctly interested in getting to know Gaia. What did all *that* mean?

Maybe, just maybe, it meant that Gaia ought to reconsider the prom. The truth was, she *liked* feeling accepted by the FOHs. It was easy enough to pretend you didn't care what those girls thought of you, especially when you knew that nothing you said or did would make you one of them, but lately they'd been warming to her. Maybe her new fear gene came special with a side of insecurity, but whatever it was, it was urging her to eke out every last possible drop of normalcy. After all, Gaia knew—maybe better than anyone—that this "real girl" stuff that she had fought so hard to acquire could disappear in a heartbeat.

And before that could happen, she was going to prom.

Her mind made up, Gaia rose, bringing her untouched food tray over to the disposal area. She dropped it on the conveyor belt, bidding a lackluster farewell to the Italian surprise, and turned to leave the lunchroom. . .

Bumping directly into Jake Montone as she did.

"Hey," she managed, quickly taking in his trim build, accentuated by a light gray sweater and jeans. The sight of her boyfriend still made her throat catch. Of course, that had been true long before she'd begun to experience fear.

"Hey," he said, slightly nervous. Clearly the awkwardness of last night's argument hadn't completely passed. "You weren't outside world lit before." He gave her a half smile that said he wasn't sure how to make things better between them, a feeling that Gaia could relate to.

"Oh, she let us out early," Gaia babbled. He had waited for her? He wanted to make up? She had dodged him all morning, not sure of what to say to compensate for the awful conversation of the night before. "Jake, I—"

"Me too," Jake agreed, cutting her off but looking visibly relieved. "I know we both said some stuff we shouldn't have said. I mean, he's your uncle, for chrissake."

Gaia was torn. Jake was obviously as eager to put last night's weirdness behind them as she was, but she got the distinct impression that Jake was telling her he forgave her for being suspicious of Oliver. The problem was that Gaia didn't want Jake to forgive her; she wanted him to understand her. She wanted him to trust her when she told him that she thought Oliver was dangerous. If Gaia and Jake were now headed toward reconciliation, it wasn't exactly on Gaia's terms.

"Jake," Gaia replied quietly, wondering even as the words came out of her mouth if she was shooting herself in the foot. "I should tell you that I meant what I said."

Jake's eyes darkened. He looked distinctly displeased with this comment. "Jeez, Gaia, here I am trying to compromise, trying to make things right again, and all you can do is stick to your paranoid point? Nice."

"No! It's just. . ." *It's just what, Gaia? It's exactly that. You had a fight with your boyfriend, and now he's trying to make up with you, and you can't even meet him halfway.* Gaia swallowed. She knew that by agreeing with Jake, she was perpetuating the misunderstanding, possibly making things substantially worse in the long run. But she couldn't bear to leave things on bad terms, and nothing short of pretending to see things his way was going to solve the problem, it seemed. "You're right. I was overreacting, and I didn't want to hear you tell me so. Let's just forget about it for now." She pasted a bright, conciliatory smile across her face.

"Don't just say that, Gaia, because you think it's what I want to hear. That's not going to get us anywhere." Jake was not to be easily placated.

So much for feminine wiles.

"Hey, don't be so serious," she chided, trying to lighten the mood. "I'm just saying, you're right. Isn't that what guys live to hear? That they're right?" She slid an arm around his waist and directed him down the hall toward their next class.

As Gaia laced his fingers through her own, he kissed her on the top of her head, sending shivers down her spine. "You're right," he conceded. "I'm a sucker for a beautiful girl telling me what I want to hear. You've figured out my weak spot." Jake was obviously more partial to a contrite and touchy-feely Gaia than to a stubborn, hard-ass Gaia, with or without fear.

Gaia allowed herself to relax as they walked down the hall. To the casual observer they looked like any other happy couple. She knew how to play the part these days; fear was good for that, at least. If she could keep it up, she'd have her wish: she'd be a normal girl with a normal—albeit amazingly hot—boyfriend.

If she could keep it up.

"I CAN'T LET YOU DO THIS."

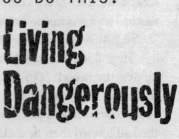

Chris Rodke looked up questioningly to see his sister gazing down at him with deadly intent. "Huh?" he asked. He couldn't imagine what he was doing that would engender such a response.

"Seriously, man. Put the fork down and step away from the surprise. Nothing good ever came from an Italian surprise," she warned, gesturing at his warmed-over lunch. He had to admit, it looked pretty unappetizing. "Surprise" was a wildly euphemistic term generally assigned to otherwise unidentifiable lunches. He and Liz were new to the Village School but not to high school life. Cafeteria food was a universal constant. "Friends don't let friends eat cafeteria food," Liz pronounced with solemnity.

"Sister, not friend," Chris corrected.

"Jeez, and after saving you from a fate worse than—or at least equal to—food poisoning," Liz griped teasingly, sliding into the seat next to him at his lunch table. "I'm feeling the love." She peeled off the lid to a container of yogurt and waved it in front of Chris's nose. "Tamper proof," she bragged.

He shrugged. "I like to live dangerously; what can I say? Besides, yogurt's, what—cultures? What the heck is a culture, and why on earth would you voluntarily ingest it?"

"I also live dangerously," Liz replied. "Actually, I've had my fill of the fast lane for today. I came ten minutes late to chem this morning. That's enough dangerous living for me."

It was true—Liz wasn't the type to miss class. "What happened?" Chris asked, genuinely curious.

"Nothing big. I got held up on my way to school."

"Long line at Starbucks?" Chris teased. Liz liked her caffeine even if, as a general rule, she had a shred more original thought process than the girls who headed there daily in gaggles.

She frowned. "Yeah, actually. But that's not what it was. I went through the park this morning on my way to school, just for a change, 'cause it was nice out."

"You shouldn't go through the park early in the

morning," Chris admonished. The hairs on the back of his neck prickled. "It's—"

"Yeah, yeah, not safe for a little girlie-girl like me. See above re living dangerously. Anyway, it was fine and totally populated. More populated than usual, in fact. That was the weirdness. There were, like, a million cops around, sort of investigating. You know, no stone unturned and all that."

Chris stiffened slightly, but his sister didn't notice. "Did they say what they were looking for?" he asked, his tone flat.

"I think they're trying to get to the bottom of the Invince business. You know, figure out who God is. They were saying that people in the park are really strung out lately—I mean, more strung out than usual. That this Invince drug is worse than anything they've ever seen because it really makes people feel immortal. So I guess they're looking for the one who's selling it."

"God," Chris echoed thoughtfully.

"Yeah." She nodded energetically, spooning up a bite of yogurt. "And there have to be people around who have seen him, who know what he looks like. You know, 'cause there are obviously a lot of people in the park who've done Invince or who know where to get it. But no one's talking."

"What did you tell them when they asked you about it?"

"What do you think I told them?" Liz asked her brother pointedly, turning her sky blue eyes on him full force.

"I told them I had no idea who they were looking for."

Life itself
was plenty
absurd on
its own.

social

pariah

IF THE GOD OF TEEN RELATIONSHIPS

Bad Vibes

was smiling down on Gaia, then the delicate balance of high school karma dictated that the god of calculus, of course, was not.

Her little scene with Jake, directly following her meltdown outside Häagen-Dazs the night before, had left her in no state of mind to worry about such trivialities as homework, but this was hardly something that she could explain to Mrs. Reingold, she of the fluffy sixties hairdo and take-no-prisoners attitude. Most of Gaia's teachers were not especially impressed by her. . . cavalier attitude toward school, to say the least. Mrs. Reingold in particular had her own hang-ups: she liked to collect assignments at the beginning of class rather than at the end—no fool, she—and she was not pleased with Gaia's extreme lack thereof. Now Gaia was on her hit list for the day.

"If you'll turn to page 176 in your textbooks," she droned, "you'll see a selection of proofs. I'd like for us to work the top three out on the board. This should be simple enough for those of you who have done the assignment." With this prediction, she glared directly at Gaia. In all fairness, Gaia had given her no reason to know that this proof would be simple enough for Gaia regardless—homework or no.

She slouched back in her seat, certain she'd be

called on to work out a proof at the board, but Mrs. Reingold nominated two other "volunteers" and Mindy White, who nearly gave herself an aneurysm, falling out of her seat, straining to be picked. *God bless her,* Gaia thought, relaxing back at her desk for the moment. Standing at the board would be tedious under the best of circumstances; she was thrilled to have a brief reprieve from her newfound social anxiety disorder.

Next to her Tammie and Megan whispered hurriedly to each other. Gaia could sense the bad vibes radiating off them in waves. She knew she'd damaged whatever currency she'd held among the FOHs when they spotted her with Liz Rodke, off to the Rodkes' mucho-exclusive black-tie affair. Gaia thought it was totally unfair that in order to fit in with one group, she was going to have to give up another. No wonder she had chosen to avoid Village School social politics up until now. It was just too exhausting trying to get the game right.

These days, though, she wanted to get the game right.

She took a calculated risk and edged her desk closer to Megan's, scraping against the linoleum floor as she did. She winced at the sound and prayed that Reingold had gone spontaneously temporarily deaf or something. "Hey," she offered tentatively.

Megan turned briefly to Gaia, eyebrows raised,

before resuming her hushed conversation with Tammie.

Denied. Okay, well, she deserved it, she supposed. Gaia was preparing to accept her lot, to turn back to the math lesson, when she decided to go for broke and make a second attempt. She had nothing to lose, right? The teacher hated her, and she was obviously a social pariah.

She leaned in again. "How weird was it running into you guys the other night?" she whispered lightly, as if bumping into the FOHs on the street was the most unexpected, most hysterically random incident in the history of random incidents. As though they didn't all live downtown, frequent the same haunts, and run into each other by accident as a general rule. "I mean, come on. Liz only asked me at the very last second, and I wasn't even going to go"—here she knew she had to tread lightly since it was obvious the other FOHs *had* in fact, wanted to go— "but Liz had an extra spot because some date had bailed on her at the last minute, and she knew I was the lame-ass who wouldn't already have plans for the night. So, you know, I grabbed the one clean thing in my closet that was even remotely right for the event and offered to help her out." Gaia felt like she'd been possessed by the spirit of a former head cheerleader. Where was this vapid banter coming from? Why was it so important to her to win these girls over?

And most importantly, was it working?

Possibly it was. Tammie regarded the deliberately frayed pockets of her stretch Seven jeans before tilting her entire desk toward Gaia, relenting. "I liked the dress," she said, in a tone that suggested she definitely *hadn't*—or at least wanted Gaia to *think* she hadn't.

No matter. Gaia found that the sarcasm was imminently preferable to being ignored. "Ugh, I wasn't sure, but really, it was all that I had. I don't get dressed up too often. It was kind of expensive, you know? Too bad that I won't have much chance to wear it again." She heard the anxiety in her voice, the please-like-me tone, but she couldn't have stopped it if she wanted to. On some base level she *needed* these girls to accept her.

Like buzzards homing in on prey, Megan and Tammie's interest was instantly recaptured. "Why not? What about prom?" Megan wanted to know. She fluttered her eyelashes at Gaia, and for the second time that afternoon Gaia found herself fleetingly wondering about the miracles of the eyelash curler.

Gaia flushed. "Yeah, totally. Prom, that would be a good place to wear it." She noticed that she was twiddling her fingers nervously and slid them under her legs to keep the external spaz-out down to a minimum. No need to go all Rain Man on these girls.

"Has Jake not asked you yet?" Tammie asked, eyes

wide with shock. "I mean, come on. *Obviously* you guys are going to prom."

"Yeah, no, I mean. . . he hasn't asked me yet."

Gaia debated how to play this. She *could* pretend it was totally normal that her boyfriend hadn't yet mentioned the biggest social event of the year or that the prom wasn't important to her. But ultimately, she determined that she was played out for the afternoon. She had no idea whether or not it was normal—though she basically suspected that it was not—but either way, maneuvering these social situations was really sucking the life out of her. *Just another example of the many ways in which I am not qualified to be a normal girl,* she thought glumly.

"Whaaat?" Tammie screeched as loud as she could without diverting Reingold's attention, which was actually pretty loud, considering. Pink Whisper stretched soft and expansive over acres of straight, white teeth. "You're *kidding.*"

Megan grabbed Gaia's hand consolingly, her French-manicured fingers light against Gaia's arm, her face the very picture of sincerity. She opened her eyes wide, resembling a cartoon kitten. "I'm *sure* he's going to ask you. Come *on.* He's just being a moron—like a typical guy."

Gaia smiled. It was comforting—more comforting than she would have thought—to be bitching about her boyfriend to her girlfriends in math class. *This* was what she'd been missing, and once she had named Jake's transgression aloud and laughed with these girls about it, she could see it for what it was—a simple oversight that would soon be corrected. And more specifically, something that every girl went through with her boyfriend at one point or another. If dealing with boyfriend-girlfriend weirdness with her friends in class was the `average teen experience,` then Gaia had arrived.

Was this what relief felt like, then?

To: megan21@alloymail.com
From: tammiejammie@alloymail.com
Re: Operation Revenge

Forget about getting back at Gaia. This thing with Jake is going to fall apart all on its own. Poor thing.

To: tammiejammie@alloymail.com
From: megan21@alloymail.com
Re: Re: Operation Revenge

   I know. And you know what? I actually feel a little bit sorry for her.

LIZ RODKE WALKED DOWN THE HALL,

Wannabe Backup Dancers

relieved to have heard the final bell of the day. English class was her favorite, but that didn't mean she wasn't ready to go home. There was only so much Samuel Beckett a girl could take in one afternoon. Life itself was plenty absurd on its own.

She was looking for Gaia. She hadn't had much chance to talk to Gaia after the party on Wednesday night, and Gaia had been acting very, well... twitchy. She'd been freakishly insecure about her dress (and it was all Liz could do to bite back an "I told you so") and hopelessly uncomfortable at the party. Liz didn't get it. From the moment they'd met, Gaia had seemed to her like a girl who could more than hold her own. It was her badass, couldn't-give-a-shit attitude that had attracted Liz to Gaia in the first place. But suddenly Gaia was jittery and unsure of herself. Liz just wanted to check in and make sure she was doing okay.

Standing on the front steps of the school entrance, she spotted Megan, Tammie, Laura, and Melanie congregated. All four wore nearly identical boot-cut, dark rinse jeans and crisp, stretchy button-downs. Like they were extras in a music video, just waiting for Avril to arrive so they could assume their positions for the line dance. No doubt headed out for some after-school group excursion from which she was excluded. It didn't matter; Liz knew this was her "punishment" for having been caught bringing Gaia to her father's party after telling the rest of the girls that she herself wasn't even invited. Whatever. She certainly wasn't going to be intimidated by a bunch of wannabe backup dancers. It would take little more than a well-directed approach to finagle her way back into their good graces. That was the beauty of dealing with a group of social lemmings. She squared her shoulders and marched over to the group.

"You guys have plans?" she asked, breaking into their circle physically and almost daring them to say no. She knew that, annoyed though they were, they weren't going to rebuff her. That wasn't the way these things worked.

"We, uh, we're going to pick up Megan's prom dress at BCBG," Laura stammered, aware of the nasty looks she was getting from her friends. No one wanted to be the girl who *wouldn't* talk to Liz—it was generally accepted that she was far too cool to be ostracized—but no one really wanted to be the one to make it easy on Liz, either. She could read them like a book—or at the very least, like a well-thumbed copy of *Us Weekly*.

"Cool. I told Chris I'd meet him. Errands for

Mom," she said, letting them off the hook. She wasn't interested in dragging her ass to SoHo, anyway. She rolled her eyes. "Parents."

The girls all laughed conspiratorially, palpably relieved to have the tension behind them. This was the signal that the social balance had realigned, that Liz was forgiven. As though the issue of her forgiveness had ever really been a question. . . . "Really," Laura agreed.

"Funny running into you the other night," Liz continued, bringing the `sore point` in question smack into the open when it was clear no one else would. "It turned out Dad had some extra tickets, and Gaia was around and free, so we decided to check it out."

"Yeah, totally, we understand," Megan said as the FOHs echoed their agreement in the background. "How could you pass that up?"

Liz grinned to herself. *Liars.* They understood. Please. They would have avoided her for days if she had let them.

"Was it fun?" Tammie asked.

"Totally. Although I'm not sure if Gaia had such a great time. She seemed a little nervous. Or maybe just bored by my dad's lame business associates and stuff." She laughed.

"Yeah, well. Gaia's got a lot on her mind lately," Megan explained, lowering her voice as if they were being watched. "I think she's worried about things with Jake."

This was news to Liz. From the little she'd seen, Jake was clearly crazy about Gaia, and though she didn't think Gaia was much for the mush factor, she could tell Gaia was equally into Jake. "What about things with Jake? I saw them in the hall before, holding hands and laughing. It sure didn't look like anything was wrong."

"I don't know," Megan answered in a singsong tone. She didn't sound especially unhappy to be the bearer of bad news. "She was talking to us in calculus, and she sounded like she might be worried. He hasn't even invited her to prom yet!" As soon as the words left her mouth, Megan dropped her head. She had obviously realized how unclassy it was for her to blurt out the nuances of Gaia's personal life to someone who had an actual investment in Gaia's emotional well-being. "I mean, that's what I heard. That she's worried."

"He gives her reason to worry," Melanie chimed in sharply. "The way he flirts with any girl with a pulse." Melanie was all too eager to cut Jake down—possibly because she felt resentful at having been passed over for someone who didn't give a crap about social politics, Liz conjectured.

"What*ever*," Tammie cut in, feigning boredom with the discussion. "The Gaia-Jake relationship debate can be continued this time tomorrow. I'm sure Liz can get the straight story herself if she's really interested. Right?" She winked at Liz. "In the meantime, we've got a dress to buy."

The FOHs turned as one unit and stalked off in the direction of Houston Street, leaving Liz to ponder the conversation. If she'd been concerned about Gaia before, now she was starting to be bona fide worried.

As
unsettling
as the
feeling was,
she couldn't
turn away
from him.

one cool chick

LIZ WAS RELIEVED TO SEE A GAIA-

Girlie Input

shaped figure emerge, finally, from the front entrance of the school. She had been waiting nearly twenty minutes since the FOHs left and was just about ready to give up when she spotted the familiar slim, muscular shadow. Messenger bag slung over one hip, perpetual look of anxious suspicion etched across her features—it was unmistakably Gaia. Liz smiled. Sure, she'd noticed a shift in Gaia's behavior since their initial meeting, but she was still one cool chick. She didn't give a crap about what anyone thought of her; at least, that was the message she gave off, wearing yesterday's cargos. And she didn't take any bull, either. Just looking at Gaia alleviated most of Liz's concerns over what the FOHs had just told her. Still, Liz did want to check in with Gaia.

Gaia peered around, hearing her name, then spotted Liz, smiled, and approached her. "Hey, what's up?" she asked, obviously pleased to see her friend. "Were you looking for me?"

"Yeah, I never got a chance to talk to you after the party; you blew out of there so fast. I wanted to make sure everything was okay."

A look of guilt flashed across Gaia's lovely features. "Yeah, I'm really sorry about that. I totally forgot that I promised Jake I would meet him later. But I should

59

have at least said goodbye. I suck." She leveled her gaze at Liz, feeling not great about the fabrication. "I had an amazing time. I'm sorry I sort of freaked out beforehand. I really appreciate that you invited me." She smiled shyly.

"Hey, no worries—I totally get it if you had to meet your man," Liz assured her. "So. . . things are good with Jake, then?" she asked tentatively. She didn't want to create a situation for Gaia that didn't exist. False alarms were never fun, and Gaia seemed so touchy these days. . . .

Gaia's face clouded over once more. "Yeah, I guess. Typical guy stuff," she explained, shrugging it off, hoping against hope that Liz didn't know her well enough to know that she knew nothing from typical guy stuff. "Megan and Tammie helped me put it in perspective."

"Megan and Tammie?" Liz probed, cocking a suspicious eyebrow. "Perspective?" Those girls wouldn't have known perspective if it hit them square in the middle of their designer-clad chests. Now Liz's inner warning bells were sounding in earnest.

"Yeah, well, I mean. . . they know that Jake can be a real flirt and that guys can be totally dense, so it was good to just get it off my chest, get some girlie input, you know?"

"Yeah, totally. I'm all for girlie input, Gaia. But those girls. . ." She sighed, arranging her thoughts in

60

her mind before she spoke. "Look, Gaia, they're obviously your friends and they're my friends, too, but I'm not sure they've always got the most, uh, *unbiased* advice to offer, that's all I'm saying. Don't put too much stock in what they have to say. They don't do too much original thinking." She hoped she didn't sound melodramatic, but she wasn't sure.

Gaia laughed. She understood what Liz was getting at, and though she wasn't about to shrug off the FOHs' friendship, however tenuous it was, it was nice to know that someone else was looking out for her. Someone who understood the murky social waters she was sailing.

"I'm serious," Liz pressed. "I don't want to go all high drama on you, but girls like that. . . well, they usually have an agenda. Just take their advice with a grain of salt," she emphasized.

Gaia's look of bemused appreciation shifted to one of mild panic. What exactly was Liz saying? Were the FOHs out to *get* her or something? Did Liz know something concrete?

Gaia's spirits sagged. The warm sense of belonging she'd had only moments ago—the acute sensation that the FOHs accepted her and that Liz cared for her—was replaced suddenly by cold dread. Jake was a flirt who had no intention of staying with her. He'd probably already asked someone else to the prom. Her "friends" were at some Starbucks downtown, plotting her social demise over nonfat lattes. Her mood, shaky as it was, deflated like a popped balloon.

"Hey," Liz broke into her thoughts softly, reading her panicked expression. "No one's conspiring against you or anything like that. It's not, you know, so dire. I'm just looking out for you because you seem a little fragile lately."

Gaia laughed shortly. Fragile. That was what she had become. If Liz only knew.

"Liz!" A booming male voice cut into their conversation. "You ready or what?"

Gaia and Liz turned simultaneously to see Skyler Rodke loping easily toward them. "Hey," he said, once he was standing before them.

"I thought Chris was meeting me." Liz sounded confused. "We were going to go pick something up for Mom uptown. Something big and heavy," she said pointedly. "It's a classic Skyler must-miss scenario."

Skyler grinned. "Chris wasn't man enough for the task. I told Mom I'd help you."

"Well, that's awfully kind of you, Your Highness, to come all the way downtown to help your poor, downtrodden sister. I'm sure the fact that there's a beautiful blond along for the ride had nothing to do with it," Liz said sarcastically.

"That's sisterly trust for you." Skyler laughed, flashing his even white teeth at Gaia. She suddenly felt flushed. Skyler was hot, no doubt about it, but it was more than that. It wasn't even that he was checking her out, because in spite of what Liz had said, Gaia didn't see it. But something about him did make her nervous.

Let's face it, just about everything makes me nervous these days, she admitted to herself. But this was a different nervous. Yet as unsettling as the feeling was, she couldn't turn away from him. She was mesmerized. She loved the fact that he was teasing her, loved the fact that he lumped her into the same group that he lumped his little sister. The vibe between Gaia and him felt familial. It was like he was the anti-Jake—unconcerned with the new bizarro Gaia's constant anxiety. Willing to take care of her. His smile was warm and inviting. She didn't share any of Liz's skepticism about his motivation for offering to help.

She shook her head. It was only a *smile*, for chrissake.

"You wanna come?" Liz offered. "Hot times at ABC Carpet are guaranteed."

Gaia smiled again but shook her head. Tempting as the offer was, whatever this magnetic draw to Skyler was, she couldn't act on it. She couldn't let Liz see her spontaneously become her older brother's lapdog. "I should be getting home. But you kids have fun."

Liz and Skyler said their goodbyes and Gaia wandered off, more perplexed by the day's events than she'd been in a good while.

From: gaia13@alloymail.com
To: jakem@alloy.com
Re: Prom

Jake—

    I know things have been a little off between us
lately; even a freak like me can tell that there's
trouble in paradise. And I'm sorry, because I take
the full blame. I've been a complete weirdo
lately, looking for reassurance and afraid of my
own shadow. Nothing like the girl you first met.
But I think we can work things out, and I think
it's worth it to try. If you can be normal, Jake,
I can be normal, too. Apparently I can be normal
and cheesy and write totally pathetic e-mails to
my boyfriend practically *begging* him not to be mad
at me so that we can go to the prom like every
other red-blooded American teenage couple. . . .

[delete]

"DAD?" CHRIS PUSHED THE DOOR TO

Verboten

his father's home office open slowly. He knew his dad was busy; after all, Dr. Rodke hardly ever worked from home. And when he was at home, the office was verboten to the rest of the Rodke clan, and it was a given that the rest of the family's activity had to be restricted to a dull roar. Chris knew he wasn't supposed to be bothering his father with anything that wasn't seriously important.

He hoped, then, that his father would agree that his news was important.

Stepping inside the office, he saw his father hunched in front of a flat-screen PC, tapping away intensely at the keyboard, wearing his lab coat for no apparent reason other than pure habit. A small microscope stood to the side of the desk. A stand containing several test tubes lay next to the microscope, small amounts of fluid slopping back and forth slowly. Chris wasn't sure what was in the test tubes, but he had an idea.

"Dad?" he repeated, suddenly less sure of the significance of his information.

His father swiveled in his ergometric chair and looked at Chris as if he were some sort of lab rat that had escaped its cage. One that wasn't really worth recapturing. "Yes?" he asked impatiently. "Can I help you with something?"

"I, uh. . ." Chris swallowed. "I don't mean to disturb you. I just wanted to tell you that the cops were questioning Liz today. In the park. This morning."

His father's level of interest instantly soared. He pushed aside the file of documents he'd been so engrossed in only moments before. "About what? Is she in some kind of trouble?"

"No, of course not," Chris assured his father, shaking his head vigorously. "Of course not," he repeated.

"Then what?"

"She was walking through the park this morning on her way to school, and the cops pulled her aside to ask her if she knew anything about Invince. About God. They were looking for leads."

His father's steely blue gaze mirrored Liz's own from lunch this afternoon. "And did she have any?"

"No, I don't think so. I mean, she hasn't bought, used, or sold any Invince, you know. So why would she know who God is?"

"Well, I don't think she would," Dr. Rodke agreed, somewhat amiably. "I don't think she would at all. Thankfully."

"She wouldn't really have any idea where Invince came from," Chris repeated, as though in a trance. "I mean, she's got nothing to do with it. But she might be coming too close." Chris revealed his true concern. True, the cops hadn't been able to get any information out of him—which was hysterical, in and of itself—and

66

they certainly weren't questioning Liz for any reason other than the fact that she'd been walking in the park this morning and had seemed the right age, the right demographic for their inquiry. But they hadn't truly had anything to link her with God. With Invince.

With Chris.

Dr. Rodke replaced the pen he'd been holding on the surface of his desk.

"Chris, Liz was asked routine questions by some semi-competent police officers who were simply doing their job. The same questions that would have been asked of anyone walking through the park this morning. As such, she wouldn't be any more suspicious than anyone else. How often do unusual things happen in Washington Square Park?" Dr. Rodke pointed out. Those were the same thoughts that Chris himself had used to rationalize the incident, but they were somehow more comforting coming from an authority figure, a doctor, a father. "There's no reason to be concerned that she is coming too close to the source of Invince. Unless there's something you aren't telling me," Dr. Rodke continued with ominous finality.

Chris shook his head again, as assertively as he was able. "No, of course not. What would I be keeping from you?"

"Good, then," Dr. Rodke stated, effectively ending the conversation. "I should get back to work. Skyler's coming by later, and we have some reports to go through. So may I suggest that you close the door behind you as you go?"

Chris was used to being dismissed. Closing the door behind himself was par for the course.

JAKE WOVE HIS WAY ACROSS THE crowded pavement of Spring Street, gracelessly sidestepping the tourists lined up the length of a city block for entrance to Lombardi's. He shook his head, annoyed. True, as one of the oldest brick-oven parlors in Manhattan, Lombardi's had earned its reputation, but **Typical High School Experience** Jake wouldn't stand on line for any restaurant in the city. Given that there was always another equally authentic, innovative, or just plain good and cheap place right around the corner, it wasn't worth it.

Besides, all of these people were in his way.

Pushing past an overweight, frizzy blond posing in front of the restaurant's awning, he pulled the rumpled e-mail printout out from the back pocket of his jeans and smoothed the paper as best as he could. *New information has been procured,* the e-mail read. *Meet me at 121 Canal Street.*

Jake hadn't known that Oliver was maintaining an outpost on Canal Street. Of course, to say that there was a lot about Oliver that he didn't know was an understatement. But it was clear that Oliver wanted to involve Jake in uncovering the threat against Gaia, and that was pretty cool. On a primary, superficial level, of course, Jake was totally worried about his girlfriend. If someone was after Gaia, he was going to go after the bastards and stop them, whatever it took. But even more than that, he liked being singled out by Oliver, liked feeling like he was a part of something bigger than the typical bullshit high school experience. Oliver was playing for real, for keeps, and Jake was glad to be on his team. So when he'd gotten the e-mail, he'd made a break for the Lower East Side without thinking twice.

"Excuse me." Frizzy was tapping his shoulder, wiping a bead of sweat off her forehead. *Damn.* That was what he got for standing still. He regarded her index finger with as much distaste as he could muster but to no avail. "Excuse me, are you from around here?"

"Uh, yeah," Jake admitted reluctantly, extending no sign of kindness or interest in helping.

"So you know the neighborhood?" She waved a guidebook under his nose, which he ignored.

"A little, yeah."

"Well, how long is the wait here usually? The book says it can be up to an hour, but that doesn't seem right." She laughed nervously, willing him to agree with her about the impossibility of it all. Her husband—or a guy Jake assumed to be her husband, judging by the matching his-and-hers Rob Me, I'm a Tourist visors perched on their heads—clapped a beefy arm across her substantial upper torso.

"Yeah, well, it's probably not right," Jake agreed, squinting over her shoulder. He thought he could make out familiar Village School figures in the distance—this was prime shopping territory, and the chicks from the Village School were champion shoppers—and he was utterly disinterested in running into anyone from school right now. He had more important things to think about.

"Right, that's what we thought," breathed the husband with a sigh of relief. "An hour. That's crazy."

Jake was already striding south and east, done with the couple. They had their guidebook, after all. "Yeah, it'll definitely be longer than an hour," he called as the light at the crosswalk changed abruptly. "More like an hour and a half."

He decided to chance it and darted across the street. Cars tended to travel down these side roads more slowly, anyway. If he hadn't been so single-mindedly focused on his mission, Jake would have seen the tourists' jaws drop in dismay. As it was, he pushed down the street briskly, completely unaware.

JAKE CUPPED HIS RIGHT HAND OVER

Spy Game Interludes

his eyes to deflect the sunlight and glanced again at the female figure across the street. In her hands she clutched a large, glossy shopping bag embossed with the BCBG label in addition to a few smaller bags from Fresh, Mavi, and a couple of other downtown boutiques. "Guys," she called, waving her bounty in Jake's direction. "Guys, is that Jake?" It was Megan, and right behind her was Laura, sucking down the final dregs of her overpriced frozen gourmet premium blend greedily and absentmindedly tossing the plastic cup into the closest garbage can with aplomb. "Uh-huh, I think so." Even over the New York traffic, he could hear their screeches loud and clear.

Normally Jake would have tried to elude them, possibly pretend he didn't see them, but it was way too late for those kinds of shenanigans. So instead he

71

turned to face them. He knew whatever expression he was making must have betrayed the fact that he was less than thrilled to be running into them, but they didn't seem at all deterred. In fact, it was with great determination that Megan led the pack across the street to where he stood. And he waited, as if without choice, tapping his foot impatiently and peering intermittently at his watch.

"I *thought* that was you!" Megan exclaimed triumphantly once they were all gathered on the same corner. "How random to run into you!"

Jake had been thinking the same thing but was much less pleased about it than Megan seemed to be. "Doing some shopping?" he asked, simply because he couldn't think of anything more interesting to say.

"Totally. I saw this really cool dress the other day and knew I had to have it for prom."

"Actually," Melanie cut in, "they had a ton of cool stuff there. At the store. Some dresses that would look amazing on Gaia. Do you know if she's picked out anything yet?" She gazed at him pointedly.

Jake blinked. Melanie obviously thought she was being discreet, but he couldn't be bothered either way. He had no idea whether or not Gaia had started looking for a dress yet. If he had to guess, he'd say no, given that she practically had to ransack her closet anytime he took her anywhere fancier than Gray's Papaya. But they hadn't even talked about prom yet.

Jake had sort of forgotten it was coming up, now that he had bigger things on his mind. And Gaia. . . well, Gaia wasn't the type to work herself into a state of neurosis about something like the prom. Or at least, she hadn't been when he'd first fallen for her. Lately he wasn't so sure. "I, uh, don't know, to be honest," he admitted. "If she has, she hasn't shown me yet."

"Ooh, maybe she wants it to be a surprise," Megan offered. "You know, like the groom not seeing the bride's dress before the wedding."

"Yeah, just like that," Melanie said witheringly. "Except this is the prom, not a wedding."

"Well, you know Gaia," Tammie oozed in a tone that could possibly be construed as less than sincere. "Whatever she wears, she'll look fabulous."

Jake grinned. "That's definitely true. I'm not too worried about it." He stole another peek at his watch. It was getting late. He couldn't waste any more time with these girls and risk making Oliver wait for him. He knew timing was everything with these little spy game interludes.

"Oh, do you have somewhere to be?" Melanie teased.

"Actually, yeah, I do," Jake replied, struggling not to reveal his impatience. "I'm in kind of a hurry. But if I talk to Gaia, I'll mention that you guys wanted to take her shopping."

"Oh, definitely," Melanie cooed. "You should definitely do that."

But whether or not she was kidding, Jake was already gone, headed down the street at practically a jog.

"WELL," MELANIE EXCLAIMED, ONCE

A Pathetic Project

Jake had disappeared down the block, "it looks like we won't have to bother with Operation Revenge after all. I guess Gaia's relationship is falling apart without us even having to interfere." She grinned nastily. "Whatever. I told her Jake was a total player." She didn't look at all sorry to be proven right.

"You think so?" Megan looked genuinely curious. "I mean, yeah, he's a flirt, and yeah, *I* definitely wouldn't mind if he was interested in taking a break from Gaia, but I don't know. . . . I mean, like we said, she has a way with guys, and he didn't act like they were on the skids."

"Why would he tell us if they were?" Laura pointed out.

"I bet they're not done yet is all," Megan said. "And to be honest, after the way she was acting in calculus, I kind of hope they're not. I actually feel a little bad for her. It looks like being a freak has finally gotten the better of her. It's like. . . she finally *cares* what we think or something. Which she should," she hurried to add. "I mean, it's about time. But I still say there's something to be learned from hanging around with Gaia Moore."

"Please," Melanie replied. "She's a total loser and completely hygienically challenged. I mean, really."

"If she hangs with us, we can help her out with that," Tammie mused. "Anyway, like Megan said, maybe it's worth a shot. She *was* being a little pathetic in class today. Come on—boyfriend trouble sucks. We've *all* been there."

"Great, just what we need. A project—a `pathetic project.`" Laura shook her head. "It's like we're in some bad eighties movie where we do a makeover on the uncool girl and suddenly she's gorgeous and steals all of our men. I mean, `cheerful dressing-room montage`? No, thanks."

"Sweetie, I've got news for you," Megan responded. "In case you haven't noticed, she's *already* stolen all of our men. We might as well bring her over to our side."

GAIA STRODE PURPOSEFULLY UP

Crime— Stopping

Seventh Avenue, headed toward St. Vincent's hospital. After the emotional roller coaster that had been her day at school, she needed some downtime, and she couldn't think of anyone more qualified to help her achieve a state of semi-Zen than Ed. She was crawling out of her skin, second guessing her every thought process, and if there was one person in her life who could calm her down, it was Ed. Ed would never mince words or play games, and she might even be able to confide in him about her newly reconfigured genetic makeup. If she didn't tell someone soon, she was going to burst.

Bursting was bad.

She paused outside Two Boots, contemplating a thick slice of Earth Mother Sicilian. She could get one for herself and something disgustingly meaty and greasy for Ed, something no doubt banned by his health care professionals. After all, she'd practically been the one to put him in the hospital—it was the least she could do. Though their friendship seemed shakier than it had once been, their mutual interest in junk food had lasting power. *The ties that bind,* Gaia thought, only semi-cynically.

As she dug into her bag to check out the money situation, though, she saw something suspicious. Nothing obvious, just a slight movement from out of the corner of her eye. Someone with less finely honed peripheral vision, someone less inclined to go about her daily business on high alert might not have noticed a thing. Gaia, however, was too well trained to play dumb. She'd had too many close encounters of her own not to know that something that *looked* fishy probably *was* fishy. She whirled around and backed up slowly, her well-worn Chucks moving soundlessly across concrete.

There. In the alley.

A young girl, probably about Gaia's age but more firmly built and solid, leaned against the brick wall of an abandoned building. The structure had probably at one point served as a corner deli, but it was obvious that the store had been vacant for a while. The pavement of the alley was littered with broken glass, cigarette butts, shredded paper, and stamped-out wads of gum. Lovely. Gaia's new friend was hunched over, her stout frame bent in such a way that her long, dark hair hung in straggly clumps over her shoulder. She was shrouded by a thick cloud of menace that was only enhanced by dark, droopy clothing and a chain connected from a loop on her belt to the sagging pocket of her torn cords. It didn't take x-ray vision to make out that the girl was leaning over someone else. Someone smaller. Someone pressed nervously against the side of the building. Someone afraid.

Gaia's throat caught. This was it. This was the type of moment that she lived for. Someone gross and greasy was threatening someone weaker. It could be a standard mugging; it could be some kind of small-potatoes drug deal. It didn't look like there was a weapon involved: the would-be assailant was clearly relying on her size advantage to overpower her opponent. But one couldn't be sure.

The blood rushed to Gaia's ears and her heart began to pound. Her fists suddenly felt clammy. Was she going to go all Pink Ranger, or was she going to freak out? Each second that passed felt like a tortured eternity. *I have to do this. I* can *do this,* she reminded herself. *I am trained for this. This is my job. God only knows what's going to happen to the smaller girl if I don't step in. This reaction I'm having, it's normal. It's just jitters. I can control it.* She tried to reason with her psyche, to call upon all of her training to reinforce confidence in herself that she was more than prepared for this moment. *I'm not scared. I'm not scared. I'm not scared,* she repeated, mantralike, in a hoarse whisper. She had to talk the fear down if she wanted to get through this and do what had to be done.

`Screw that. I'm terrified.`

She heard a muffled yelp from the alley and saw the larger girl bend farther forward. Based on her stance, Gaia could see that she had the smaller girl's wrist in her meaty hand and was twisting. That was it. That was the final straw. Gaia's indignation overpowered her fear.

In a flash she leapt halfway down the alley, landing, Jackie Chan style, just behind the assailant. She stepped one foot in front of Large's right leg and reached her right arm out, grabbing hold of the intertwined hands. Using all of the force of the right side of her body, she jerked her hand forcefully, causing the thwarted criminal to let go of her victim and flipping her over in an instant.

As soon as Large hit the ground, Gaia stepped squarely over her. "Back off," she growled, hoping like hell that her rapid-fire heart palpitations weren't actually audible. Inside her head, the sound was deafening.

The diminutive victim—a mousy, washed-out blond who couldn't have weighed more than ninety-five pounds—took the opportunity to bolt. She dashed down the alley at warp speed without so much as a thank-you to her savior, who was doing her best at the moment to avoid turning pale.

Gaia was used to passing out after a massive physical exertion. This didn't qualify. The waves of blurriness that danced before her eyes could only be attributed to her fear, she knew. This hadn't been a fight, had barely been more than a scuffle. She wasn't having a blackout, she was having a spaz-out, like a typical girlie-girl scared out of her wits. *Be careful what you wish for,* she thought fleetingly, unamused by the irony of the situation. She squelched the spaz urge as best she could, managing to squawk in what she hoped was a vaguely threatening tone, "Pick on someone your own size."

Large responded with an unimpressed grunt but didn't make the mistake of trying to move or otherwise overpower Gaia. She turned her head to one side, looking away and obviously willing Gaia to be off, finally. The crisis had been averted.

Gaia's heartbeat finally slowed. The immediate threat had passed. This girl wasn't going to fight back. She could do this. She was prepared for this. It was a calculated risk, and it had worked. She exhaled deeply, relieved.

She turned on her heel to leave, to resume the day's events as though they'd never been briefly interrupted by `superhero crime-stopping pursuits`. As she stalked out of the alley, though, she couldn't help but glance back over her shoulder. Thankfully, Large was making no attempt to rise from the pavement. But Gaia noticed something she hadn't seen before. A glint of color against the black-and-gray asphalt.

Slowly, cautiously, she edged back toward the scene of the crime. Leaning forward, she could now make out a colored piece of paper flattened against the ground. It almost looked like the tattoo prizes that could be found in the bottom of a Cracker Jack box. She knelt down and peeled the paper up into her hand with her fingernail, studying the image more closely. A strand of hair that had escaped her ponytail during the scuffle dropped into her line of vision and she pushed it impatiently back. The illustration was unmistakable. It was a small square of white paper, and just in the center, gleaming brightly at her, were four perfect renderings of a bright, vivid polka dot. Instantly Gaia realized what she held in her hand, what she was looking at. And instantly a feeling of dread overtook her.

Oranges.

Ed had no idea who this hot-and-cold **gender dynamics** mannequin was.

FOR THE THIRD TIME THAT AFTERNOON

The Order of the Day

Jake retrieved the crumpled e-mail printout from the back pocket of his jeans, smoothed it out as much as was possible at this point, and squinted at the address. *121 Canal Street.* He stared again at the simple white door that stood before him. One twenty-one, no doubt about it. He inhaled deeply. The air was heady with exhaust fumes, exotic cooking spices, and ripe garbage from an overflowing trash can that stood at the corner of the sidewalk. All in all, the location was thoroughly unimpressive. But Jake knew enough about Oliver by this point to know that nondescript was the order of the day. The door before him was shabby and splintering and looked like something that would have crumpled at even the slightest tap, but there was a reason that Oliver had provided him with a door code. Jake knew it would have been literally impossible to infiltrate the rickety-looking walk-up without it.

Carefully Jake punched a set of numbers into a touch pad that had been installed in the outer doorway. He had a moment of wavering doubt, but when he jimmied the doorknob and shoved lightly against the door with his hip, it gave way with only slight resistance. He stepped into the entryway of the building, which was no more impressive on the inside. "Hello?" he called out.

There was no answer. Of course. Oliver's instructions had been very specific: he'd been told to proceed directly to the third floor. Jake made his way up the warped, unsteady staircase, taking pains to avoid the odd glue trap that had been left out. Thankfully, the traps were all empty. Small favors and all that. Though he was fairly certain mice would be the least of his concerns today.

The third-floor landing didn't appear to hold much promise: the floor was dusty and hadn't been swept in. . . well, hadn't been swept in a while. More mousetraps were tossed to the far corners of the hallways, collecting lint, which was slightly preferable to the alternative, considering. But the door directly to Jake's left was clearly marked 302, which was exactly where Oliver had promised he'd be waiting. Jake knocked uncertainly, then decided that Oliver wouldn't be moved by his indecision. Oliver preferred a man who knew his own mind. Jake stepped more confidently through the door.

He was greeted immediately with the sight of Oliver's back. The room was small and bare, furnished only with an ancient floor lamp radiating minimal light from a naked bulb, a wooden desk that had seen better days, and an office chair that could easily have been swiped from the street. It was missing a wheel, Jake noticed. But at the desk Oliver was punching furiously at the keypad of a state-of-the-art iMac, barely taking note of Jake's arrival. Jake knew Oliver well enough to know that his `nonreaction` to his guest's arrival was one part intimidation tactic, one part intense span of attention. Sweat stood out on his brow, and his gaze was locked in fierce concentration.

"Hey," Jake said. His voice sounded too loud. "Five-thirty. I'm here. What have you got?"

"Shhh!" Oliver reprimanded, tapping out a final thought and slamming down on the control key. Then, as if remembering his initial invitation, he swiveled in his chair to face Jake. "Oh, yes," he said by way of greeting. "I'm glad you could make it."

"Wouldn't miss it," Jake replied easily, coming closer to catch a glimpse of the computer screen. It was devoid of anything especially `juicy,` but he could tell that Oliver had been sending out a flurry of e-mails just as Jake arrived. "You've got info on the bastards after Gaia?"

"Yes, of course. Some of my sources have intercepted various messages. . . . Look here." He pointed at the screen. "'Imperative for testing that further samples be taken from the subject for hair follicle tests. A few strands will be sufficient, but a dozen will be more useful. . . .'" He scrolled down the screen, continuing to read select passages aloud. "'Confrontation with the subject should be kept to a minimum.'" He turned from the screen and back to Jake, his face impassive. Jake could tell Oliver expected him to make something of the passages he'd just read. Too bad he was stumped.

Jake's forehead wrinkled in concern. "So you're saying Gaia's the subject?" That much was pretty clear. Why else would that information be of any interest to Oliver?

"Well, we can't be sure, but I should expect so."

"But you don't know who is after her?"

"No real leads, I'm afraid," Oliver said ruefully, clasping his hands on his knee. "But this e-mail exchange in and of itself only serves as confirmation of my suspicions. It can hardly be denied that someone is after her. We just need to determine who."

"Do you think the answers might be in her computer?"

Oliver barked a short, quick laugh. "What were you thinking? That we'd just hack into her laptop? Don't you think she'd realize if you'd been at her private files?"

Jake flushed. "You're right, of course. I always forget who I'm dealing with." Of course Gaia would notice if Jake had somehow just run off with her computer. His delusions of Bond were getting the best of him.

"It's easy enough to do so. We've all underestimated Gaia at one point or another."

"But not you. You never did."

Oliver cleared his throat and leaned back in his chair. "You give me too much credit. I have, at times, underestimated her. But I learn from my mistakes." He gazed wistfully at the wall, momentarily lost in thought. It could have been Jake's imagination, but was Oliver slightly uncomfortable with the direction the conversation was taking?

"Now, then," Oliver said brusquely, snapping back to attention and hastily straightening a disorganized pile of papers that lay scattered next to the computer. "Your job should be simple enough, especially given your relationship with Gaia. I merely want you to keep an eye on your girlfriend—a closer watch than before, given this new piece of information." He began to tap a pen against the desk rhythmically. "I imagine you wouldn't mind that."

Jake laughed. "Nah, that shouldn't be too painful. But are you sure there isn't anything more—?"

"You were hoping for what? Espionage? Deep undercover? Disguises? Fancy toys? Not just yet, my friend. There's no need for anything more than active surveillance. I want you to report back any suspicious behavior, anything odd or off—even something Gaia herself might say or do."

Jake thought back to Gaia's panicked indictment of Oliver the night before, her uncharacteristically clingy behavior in school. That was definitely suspicious behavior—but he worried that he'd sound like a real jackass "reporting" that his girlfriend was too *into* him lately. No, he'd take a watch-and-wait approach before reporting that, for sure. He wanted something more concrete. Something that seemed less, well, *Jake*-centric. Something less easily dismissed as ego. "Do you think it's someone at the boardinghouse?" he asked suddenly. Anything was possible, after all—he was learning this fast.

"Doubtful. The boardinghouse is run by top Agency officials."

"But infiltration would be possible, right?"

"Possible, yes. But unlikely. However, I see no reason why the boardinghouse shouldn't fall under the scope of your surveillance. Just don't concentrate too much of your effort there."

"What about the Droogs? That's the new threat in town. Do you think IV could have anything to do with whoever's after Gaia?"

A flash of consternation flickered across Oliver's face, but when he spoke, he was composed. "Absolutely not. Droogs are simply immature thrill seekers who've run out of ways to pass time. I can't think of anything less likely to be connected to Gaia. Don't waste our time with such trivialities, Jake."

Jake was instantly contrite. "You're probably right. I'm sorry. I was just, you know, trying to open my mind to every possibility. But yeah, I'll just stick close to Gaia. That'll be the best plan for now."

Oliver fixed Jake with a measured smile. "Indeed. A sharp eye on Gaia is really all that we need."

The boy's eagerness can work both with me as well as against me. True, he is confident almost to a fault—some might say arrogant—and ready to take on whatever task I may give to him. True, he has proven himself in the field. He is strong and physically capable, and his loyalty to Gaia is impressive indeed. I can think of no one better suited for the act of surveillance, particularly given his neophyte status. Jake Montone is far too inexperienced to come close enough to learning the truth.

Although. . . he has demonstrated that he yearns to be at the center of the action. He wants to know all there is to know. He courts danger, even more than he is aware. He will ask questions, and I must cover my own tracks and shield my own suspicions. He cannot learn more than I am ready to reveal. He must work with me, for me, on my timeline, or he is useless to me. . . and to Gaia.

Jake believes that our interest lies in protecting Gaia, and
he is right. I would sooner poison myself than see her hurt at
the hands of another. But there
are other factors involved. It
may be that someone is after
Gaia due to her unique gifts. It
may be that someone has learned
of her genetic composition.
Someone may wish to harness her
power, to learn from it, to
replicate it. And though I said
otherwise to Jake, that someone
may have leaked a dangerous
chemical onto the black market,
this Invince, this drug that
makes people think they are
immortal. It is a wild card, an
element of uncertainty that
threatens to unravel my careful
efforts. This I cannot allow. No
one will have my niece under a
microscope, examining her like a
laboratory rat and manipulating
her biochemistry for their own
benefit. I will not have it.

As her uncle, Oliver would not

have Gaia the subject of a nefar-
ious science experiment.

Loki, that old, comfortable
companion, agrees.

If anyone is to benefit from a
study of Gaia Moore, it will be me.

ED WAS PLEASED TO NOTE THAT THE

Ultimate Strangeness

doctor leaning over him, clipboard in hand, was humming. Humming had to be good news. There was no way a doctor would be so cruel as to exhibit such unrelenting exuberance if he didn't have something key to pass along to Ed.

Such as, for example, a discharge notice. A clean bill of health.

Ed had been in and out of hospitals more than he cared to reflect on ever since his skateboard accident a few years ago, and while he had by now gotten used to the sterile, antiseptic atmosphere, it didn't mean he was eager to set up short-term residence at St. Vincent's. The stack of extreme sport magazines piled up on his nightstand was as homey as he wanted the room to be. He wasn't interested in being on a first-name basis with each and every staff member, no matter how friendly they were to him. No, he'd be thrilled to return to his parents' apartment—and maybe even willing to allow them to shower him with embarrassing amounts of affection. Or at the very least, a decent meal. The cookie Kai had brought him was the closest he'd come to actual sustenance in days.

And it had, evidently, done wonders toward nursing him back to health. The doctor took a quick listen with his stethoscope (which Ed was fairly convinced was actually just a prop), clapped Ed on the shoulder, and sat back on the edge of the bed. "Well, son, I gather you're ready to leave?" the doctor asked, eyes twinkling.

"Definitely. What sort of time frame are we talking about?" There had been discussion of leaving that evening, but Ed didn't want to hold his breath.

"How quickly can you pack up?"

"Man, are you kidding? That's awesome." He wasn't going to *have* to hold his breath. Excellent.

"We've called your parents. They'll be here in an hour or so to check you out and take you home. There are some papers they need to fill out for you to be released. In the meantime, you can collect your belongings. And do let me know if you need anything else." The doctor smiled, readjusted his stethoscope, and left the room, leaving the door slightly ajar.

Ed really didn't have too much to pack; he'd just change back into the clean set of clothes his mother had left for him. He'd already read and reread all of the magazines more times than he'd wanted to—they were more than ready for the recycling bin. But there was no pressing need to leap out of bed and get to gathering, so he lay back for a moment, thinking. Reveling in the thought of returning home.

The door squeaked open again and Ed turned toward it, thinking the doctor had forgotten one semi-vital piece of information—some nonparental form to be filled out, probably. But he was wrong.

Instead it was Gaia, looking more disheveled than usual. Of course, even in this condition she was a vision to Ed, but he was instantly concerned nonetheless. Who wouldn't be? Her jeans were streaked with dust and she had a scratch on one cheek. She was flushed and her hair hung in sweaty straggles. Her hooded sweatshirt was slightly askew. "Hey," she said softly.

"Hey," Ed said, glad to see her. He figured he'd let her warm up to telling him what had happened. He knew better than to push with Gaia. "I'm getting sprung today. In an hour, actually. You're just in time."

She beamed at him, her entire face lighting up. "Really? That's great. I'm so glad you didn't have to stay longer." She came around to the side of the bed and lowered herself into one of the two plastic visitor chairs that stood beside it. "I'm really, really glad that you're okay," she said, her voice grave.

"Of course I'm okay! Don't overreact. Seriously— surface wounds," Ed joked. It was obvious that something was bothering Gaia. There was something she was trying to to tell Ed. But she was having trouble getting it out. "Gaia," Ed said insistently, "is there something on your mind?"

"I could have stopped it," she blurted.

"What do you mean?" asked Ed.

"I mean I was headed towards the park that night. I ran into the thugs that attacked you. But I didn't do anything to stop them."

Ed was silent for a moment. Whatever suspicions he'd had about Gaia's behavior were now confirmed. Her skittish behavior at their last meeting was definitely suspect. She'd been timid and twitchy—one hundred percent nerve endings. Not that every walking piece of scum was anyone's responsibility, let alone hers. She'd definitely exceeded term limits as self-appointed teen vigilante at large. But as far as Ed knew, Gaia had never seemed to be on the receiving end of that particular memo, so he could only guess that something was deeply wrong with her. Still, he had no intention of making her feel bad about what had happened. There was no way she could have known who those thugs would end up hurting.

"Gaia, don't be ridiculous. You've really got to get over this Buffy complex. I mean, you could also stop, um, gingivitis if you were willing to floss after every meal. I know you're, like, superhuman, but you can't prevent every bad thing, ever. I know you did what you could."

"I should have stopped it," she said, more to herself than to Ed.

The more Ed thought about it, the more it did weird him out that Gaia hadn't stopped the attack. The Gaia he knew and—hell, just admit it—loved totally wouldn't have let any of those punks get by. Something was up with Gaia, but Ed didn't know how to go about probing without seeming suspicious.

He wondered, fleetingly (and not for the first time), if whatever was going on in Gaia's world had anything to do with the bizarre CIA visit to Heather. He contemplated mentioning that, asking her if she had done any follow-up, but at the last minute he chickened out. One look at her unkempt appearance suggested that now wasn't exactly the time. Gaia was acting so strange, so un-Gaia-like, that he didn't want to do anything to push her buttons.

He was started out of his thoughts by the sound of a pronounced sniffle. He glanced up to see what had to be the ultimate strangeness he'd ever encountered.

Gaia was crying.

She was pretending that she wasn't—staring off in the opposite direction of the bed and dabbing at her eyes methodically—and she was definitely trying to stifle the tears, but there was no denying that actual wetness was emanating from her eyes. Ed blinked. This had to be a first for them. In all that he had been through with Gaia, he didn't think he had *ever* seen her cry.

He sat up straight in bed, reaching out to her. "Hey—don't worry. I told you, I know that you did what you could, and you know, here I am, totally fine. They're letting me go. No permanent damage. No worries. And I don't blame you, so please don't blame yourself."

Gaia rubbed at her eyes but didn't say anything in response. After a moment she abruptly turned back to Ed. "Forget it, I'm being a spaz." And just as soon as the tears had begun, they were locked away again. It was like spontaneous bipolar disorder or something.

"So other than your great escape, what else is new? Have you made plans for prom yet?"

Ed was starting to wonder if he had somehow stumbled into the twilight zone. What the hell was up with this non-Gaia—first the unnecessary levels of self-flagellation, then the spontaneous crying jag, and then the less-than-subtle subject change? Granted, Gaia had never been an open book, but they were plumbing new depths of odd behavior. And since when did Gaia Moore care about things like *prom*?

"Uh, no plans yet. I guess I'm the last one to deal with it, huh? Probably all anyone can talk about at school?"

"Yeah, just about. There's a lot of speculation that the IV crimes will get in the way of the big night—but I don't think the students will really let that happen." She wrapped a thick rope of hair around one finger pensively. "So, you're thinking of going, right? Who are you going to ask? Kai?"

Ed shrugged. "Who knows? I mean, she's really laid

back, you know, so I think we could probably go as friends and she'd be cool with it. But I guess I'll have to see. She might have had a more romantic evening in mind." He thought for a moment. "I'll probably have to figure it out sooner rather than later, right? I mean, whoever I end up going with will want to have time to get a dress, or schedule a hair appointment, or. . ." He peered at Gaia inquisitively. "What *is* it you girls do for the big night?"

Gaia grinned self-consciously. "Hey, you're the one who dated the self-proclaimed style queen," she pointed out. "But yeah, I think dress shopping is a big thing. I'm thinking of hiring someone. Like, a consultant for the fashionably impaired. Think they do charity cases for free?"

"Gaia—God, what is up with you lately? Since when do you *care* about stuff like that?"

Gaia's face crumpled. "I'm kidding. But it would be nice to see how the other half lives for once," she retorted. "So I want to go to prom. Is that such a big deal?" She crossed her arms defensively.

"No, no, you're right, I'm a jerk. It's just a surprise," Ed relented. Gaia being defensive, he could handle. But Gaia being defensive about *prom* was *muy* twilight zone. He backpedaled, aiming for damage control. "So I take it Jake Montone is the lucky man? Your escort for the evening?"

Gaia paused for a moment, as though missing a

beat. When she spoke, she sounded tentative, but if she had doubts about Jake, she wasn't saying. "Yeah. Should be fun," she said shortly.

Ed had no idea who this hot-and-cold mannequin was who'd replaced his best friend/ex-girlfriend/whatever the hell she was. He could tell that she was keeping something from him, but he had no idea how to bring it out. Direct confrontation wasn't the way—she was too edgy these days. He decided to take a gamble and spill one of his own secrets. "I'll tell you something if you promise not to say anything."

She flashed him a you've-gotta-be-kidding look. Who would she tell? "Uh, yeah. Promise."

"I, uh, actually kind of wish I could bring Heather. You know, for old times' sake," he clarified. "I think she'd really like to be there, and I feel bad that she won't be able to go. I mean, I feel bad about everything, you know, with her. I think we could have had fun."

Ed knew Gaia understood. She and Heather had come to understand each other after all they'd been through. When Gaia had visited Heather in the hospital, they had really bonded. Ed knew that Gaia could relate to his feelings of nostalgia.

"Yeah, Heather was definitely born for prom." Gaia chuckled. "I'm sure she'd love to go."

"Yeah," Ed agreed. He didn't mention that as a general rule, he wasn't especially impressed by girls who were born for prom. When Ed and Heather had been together, what he'd liked most about her was the side of her that her clotheshorse friends didn't get to see (and probably wouldn't have appreciated if they *had* seen). And ever since the second go-round with Heather, his standards were even higher. Kai's open, friendly personality and adorable, skater-trendy looks weren't even enough for him. Maybe he'd been sort of reverse spoiled by Gaia. Maybe he needed someone who posed a constant challenge, someone who never let things lie, someone who was always, somehow, steeped in adventure. . . . *Crap,* he thought. *Maybe I won't ever be satisfied with a normal girl.*

"But the more I think about it. . . maybe you should ask Kai," Gaia broke in, as if thinking aloud. "Heather might feel uncomfortable back at the Village School, with everything that's. . . happened. And you and Kai would definitely have fun. But you should ask her soon. You're too good of a guy to string her along until the last minute." She gazed steadily at him, an intimate knowledge and affection written across her features. Though when Gaia had brushed up on her knowledge of gender dynamics was a further mystery to him.

Ed sighed, wishing he could muster up more enthusiasm for the pseudorelationship he had some-how fallen into. "Yeah," he replied. "I guess I am."

So Ed and Kai are going to the prom as friends. That's cool.

Really. Ed's had a hard time, after everything that happened with Heather and the accident. I know that a lot of his friends freaked when he was in a wheelchair, didn't know how to deal, blew him off. He went from being "Shred" Fargo, daredevil skate rat, dating the most popular girl in school, to pretty much being a social pariah. I mean, no one wants to date the guy in the wheelchair. Or you know, even maneuver their way through a few awkward conversations to steer things back to usual. So that had to really suck for him, just to understate things a bit.

I think that's why he and I connected at first. We both knew what it was like to be singled out, to be the weird one, the person that's a little different, that no one knows how to handle. We were both used to being avoided or ignored. And so when I

tried to use my typical emotional
defense tactics against him, he
saw through my BS and wouldn't
take it. So of course I think
he's great. A great catch.
Probably my best friend and definitely one of my *only* friends.
And, as established, I'm not
exactly one for winning friends
and influencing people.

I have no doubt that a relationship never would have worked
out between us. For starters,
I've proven completely incapable
of the typical John-Hughes-movie-
style high school romance. The
closest I've ever gotten to true
cheese was when Ed handed me a
big, honking wheel of it on one
of our dates. He was joking, of
course, but he knew. He knew I
needed help in the cheese depart-
ment. A cheese tutorial.

Then there's also the fact
that anyone I date for more than,
oh, twenty-four hours finds their
life in jeopardy. And I'm not
being melodramatic. I wish to God
I were. Ed knew this and was

willing to cope with it, but I couldn't do that to him. He was just too vulnerable, and I care about him too much. I couldn't see the same thing happen to him that happened to Sam.

So if Ed's single right now, then Kai is pretty much the perfect prom date. She's cute, she's fun—as far as I can see—and she clearly likes him a lot. And she's probably at least a little interesting, because I don't think Ed could hang out with her if she wasn't.

And most of all, she's *normal*. In a way that Ed hasn't seen in a while, in a way that he deserves. She probably won't be on the run from some ancient enemy of her father's with a killer eye for sharpshooting, and she probably won't try and manipulate him financially or emotionally or expect him to be anything he's not. She's probably perfect for him. You know, as a normal, no-strings-attached, let's-hang-out-after-school-and-chill friend.

And since Ed is my best
friend—let's face it, the closest
thing to a true soul mate that
I've known, someone who understands me beyond the surface
chemistry that often brings two
people together—then of course, I
want him to have that. A stable
friend, without questions or
drama.
    Which so isn't me.
    So I'm cool with it. Really.
    Damn.

Okay. Just when I think that 1) Gaia can't get any stranger, or 2) I've gotten so accustomed to her strangeness that it isn't going to faze me anymore, some new form of weirdness comes and resets the charts, blows all of my theories to hell, forces me to update the Gaia files.

Gaia Moore is worried about prom? Screw that—Gaia Moore is *interested in attending the prom?* I mean, I know that when we were dating, we took some baby steps toward standard dating proce- dures, and I'm not naïve enough to pretend that she and Jake don't have at least some basic working knowledge of male-female relations, but still.

This is all very odd.

It's as if she's been pos- sessed by the spirit of Heather Gannis—which I'm not saying is such a bad thing. Just radically unexpected.

Gaia wants to go to prom. Gaia worries that she won't be asked.

Gaia wonders what she'll wear.
Gaia stresses over Jake. Gaia
cries?

I'm baffled, truly.

I have to say, though, that
this alternate universe into
which we've stumbled makes me
think twice. What would it be
like to be dating this new Gaia?
She might, for example, be more
willing to expose herself to me
(emotionally. Expose herself emotionally, I mean). Would she be
more open to honesty and inti-
macy? Less afraid of being depen-
dent? All of those issues that
burdened our relationship. . .
would they just be. . . gone?

Probably not. I mean, people
don't just undergo entire personality transplants overnight
(except for Heather, but, well,
there were extenuating circumstances in that case). Gaia's
just too. . . *Gaia*. It wouldn't
work between us. No way.

Good thing I've got that
straight.

restored
to red-
blooded,
daredevil,
heartthrob
status

date
for
the
prom

INEXPLICABLY, GAIA FELT AN

Remedial Fear Management

overwhelming rush of relief on stepping through the automatic doors of St. Vincent's and back out onto the street. The air was no fresher than it had been on her journey to the hospital, but at least she was outdoors. Her conversation with Ed had left her feeling panicky, like she was suffocating—a sensation that was fast becoming all too familiar. She inhaled deeply, reveling in the slight release of tension, hastily resuming normal breathing patterns once she realized, again, that a New York City street corner wasn't exactly the great outdoors.

She shrugged, turned on her heel, and started off in the direction of the boardinghouse. She glanced briefly at her watch. It wasn't too late, actually; there might even be an hour or two of shopping left. She wondered fleetingly about calling Liz. Didn't other girls give their friends a call whenever they felt like it, just to hang out? Couldn't they manage simple, casual, teenage social graces? Gaia's head spun. Logically, she knew she was wasting precious emotional energy obsessing about something mundane.

But she couldn't stop.

She gritted her teeth. She had known that there

would be a downside to experiencing fear. She'd expected to feel more nervous, possibly more anxious, and of course a little more cautious in the face of battle. But what she *hadn't* counted on was this all-consuming anxiety. Was this *really* what other people went through every day? Second guessing every gesture and action, no matter how inconsequential? She didn't think so. Other people had years of practice managing their emotions, their insecurities. They had learned to prioritize the real concerns and rationalize those that were merely a hindrance to basic human functioning. Gaia, conversely, needed some sort of crash course. Remedial fear management. Ha. Did they offer that at the Learning Annex? Was she going to have to sign up for industrial-level therapy? The idea made her giggle nervously—she wasn't sure it was such a joke. Or if it was a joke, she wasn't sure how funny it was.

Turning down a quiet side street, she was startled by the sound of breaking glass. Glancing to her right, she was shocked to see three thuggy-looking boys—she thought the oldest was no more than fifteen, max—swinging something heavy and blunt at the basement-level window of a brownstone.

Having spent so many evenings in Washington Square Park, it was rare for the sight of petty crime to surprise Gaia, but this—obviously an attempt to break into a private residence—was new. This was amazingly ballsy. This was *broad daylight.* Yes, it was a slightly quieter side street of the West Village, and yes, there weren't a ton of people out and about, but really. She literally couldn't believe her eyes. Either the boys genuinely hadn't noticed her or they had noticed her but didn't find her to be a threat.

Her heart jumped into her throat. A big part of her hoped that the boys hadn't seen her, would just go about their business, not bothering her if she didn't bother them. But another part of her—the part that actually remembered fearlessness—couldn't just let this go. She had no idea what these boys were up to: it could be an intended burglary, or it could be something more benign—low-level vandalism, cheap thrills, or something. . . . But she found that she couldn't walk away, despite the adrenaline coursing through her system at warp speed. She'd already survived one battle today. Heck, she'd more than survived—she'd triumphed. She knew, intellectually, that she could do this. It was mainly an issue of getting her emotions on board.

She sized the boys up mentally. All three were crouched over the window, bashing the remaining shards of glass with whatever object happened to be handy. The smallest was wiry and young looking. His shredded tan cords were hanging low, and Gaia could practically count the knobs of his lower spine through the pale strip of skin that was exposed. His two partners were bigger, but not by much. One wore a backward baseball cap that had seen better days and dusty black cargos. The other, the one she had presumed to be the oldest, sported a crew cut and a worn concert T-shirt. The Grateful Dead. How original. Like this kid was even old enough to have seen them perform the first time around....

The Deadhead was the likely ringleader since he was, as quietly as possible while still using an authoritative tone, prodding the other two. "There, you got it, dude!" he exclaimed, as though pleasantly surprised that the window was, in fact, demolished. "We're in." He paused contemplatively. "D'ya think there's an alarm?" The other two nodded as though they'd been thinking the exact same thing. Gaia herself had been wondering this, but they'd been at the window for a while, so if the cops were going to come, she figured they would already have arrived.

No alarms, then. It was all up to her. There was that intellectual thought process again, the one that begged her emotions to come along for the ride.

You can do this, she told herself. *You've done it literally hundreds of times. Chances are, all you'll need to do is put a scare in them, anyway.* She realized that her palms were clenched tightly and that she was sweating profusely. *Thank you, fear.* She forced herself to work it out: all she had to do, she knew, was take out the Deadhead. Once he was overpowered, his sad little cronies would surely fall into line. And since they had their backs to her and were infinitely consumed with their work, she had the element of surprise working in her favor, in addition to her years of training. She willed her trembling limbs to steady and thought back to this afternoon, how she'd been able to break up the mugging with relatively little difficulty. It didn't matter that she was terror girl these days. Frightened or not, she still had to bust a little ass kicking.

She tiptoed up behind Deadhead and swiftly wrapped an elbow around him, yanking him backward in a forceful headlock. "Hey, wha—," he cried in alarm.

"I don't know what you losers are doing, but it's not going to happen," Gaia growled. She could hear the nervous lilt to her voice and didn't like the sound of it. She struggled to contain her emotions.

"Let me go," Dead yelled, obviously forgetting all about causing a scene. That wouldn't do. Gaia didn't want the cops to come any more than he did. Cops would only lead to questions that she wasn't prepared to answer.

"Shut *up*—," she ordered as one of the others whacked her in the back of her knees with whatever they'd been using to break the window. It was a cheap trick, and she crumbled like a sack of potatoes. *Focus, Gaia, focus,* she commanded herself. She rolled to her right and swept her legs around, tripping and toppling Dead. Using the momentum of the roll, she leapt back to her feet, crouching into a ready position.

"Yo, what are you *on*, bitch?" Cargo Pants snarled, which was ironic given that the chances that he was high far outweighed the chances that she was. He lunged at her, and she grabbed his arms and wrestled him to the ground. Clinging to her elbows, he flipped them over in tandem so that he had her pinned. He hauled off and slammed down, missing her nose by inches.

Gaia tilted her head, absorbing the impact on her cheek. Her head ricocheted off the pavement and her ears rang. *That can't be good,* she thought briefly. She was losing ground—losing the fight—fast. Out of the corner of her eye she saw that the smallest was creeping closer. Mustering a burst of reserve energy, she drew her legs into her chest and released with full force, the flats of her feet connecting solidly with his lower shins. He fell to the ground, clutching his legs and moaning. "Let's get out of here," he whimpered.

Dead's eyes darted back and forth along the block. "Yeah. Someone definitely heard this. We gotta get out of here before the cops come." He glared menacingly down at Gaia, picking himself up slowly and dusting his jeans off. "You got lucky, girl. We hafta hit the road." He spat by way of punctuation.

114

She glared at him as ominously as she could. "Lucky, my ass."

But the boys were already over it. They'd gathered their bag of tricks—whatever was in it was *seriously* heavy, Gaia knew firsthand, but they snatched it up and scampered away.

She exhaled slowly. Her ribs hurt, and she guessed a bruise was already forming on her cheek. But she'd stopped the burglary or whatever it was. That was something.

And oh, yeah. That level of exertion required to cause a total failure of Gaia's system? The one that dictated that she pass out after any scuffle? `Yeah, still fully functional.` Before she could attempt to clear her head and drag her weary body to a semi-safe location, the familiar darkness set in and the world dropped away.

Memo

From: L
To: Team U
Re: Genesis

Subject spotted downtown intercepting a breaking
and entering. As per the norm, subject rendered
unconscious by exertion.

Subject is not to be harmed under any
circumstances. Order full-time surveillance,
protection when necessary.

No one will hurt her.

ED HEARD THE DOORBELL RING BUT

Basic Human Niceties

couldn't bring himself to rush to answer it. He knew his mother would race for the door, anyhow. She was so thrilled to have walking, talking, dating, and heck—even convalescing Ed back home that she didn't mind taking care of him in these small ways. Ed knew she'd be ecstatic to open the door to his "cute little girlfriend" and show Kai to his room. It didn't matter how many times he told her that he and Kai had broken up; Ed's mother was determined to imagine her son's teenage experience to be idyllic. Short-term paralysis notwithstanding, of course.

He was being bitter, he knew. The entire time he'd been wheelchair bound, he had resented his parents and his sister for being awkward and strange around him. Somehow they'd been embarrassed by his handicap, and since Ed himself was having a hard enough time dealing with it, he could have done with some more support from them. But it had never come.

Now, though, his parents couldn't dote on him enough. His sister, when she was home, cooed over him and teased him about what a lady-killer he'd become. She didn't seem to notice that he and Kai had regressed to the realm of the platonic. And every time the phone rang or someone came to the door for Ed, the Fargos took it as another personal victory. They had won their son back from the land of the ill and disfigured.

Today was no exception. "Why, hello, Kai!" he could hear his mother trilling, a shade too enthusiastically. *Quelle* Donna Reed. Her shrill voice echoed off the tiles of the front hallway. "How *nice* of you to stop by! Ed's just gotten back—he's in his bedroom."

It was a sure sign that they still, on some level, considered him an invalid: they had no qualms about sending girls straight to his bedroom. Maybe they were hoping they'd catch him in the throes of a passionate make-out session—proving his "recovery" complete, once and for all.

Come to think of it, it would be a fun theory to prove. Too bad there weren't any real, viable contenders these days.

There was a hearty rap at the door, followed by his mother's energetic singsong once again. He wondered if that level of perkiness was exhausting to her to maintain. "Ed? Ed, guess who's here?"

"I can't imagine," he mumbled to himself, softly enough that neither Kai nor his mother would hear from the other side of the door.

The doorknob turned and the door slid open to reveal his mother's beaming face. "Ed, dear, you have a visitor. Are you up for it?" Wide, watery eyes told him she expected that he would be. She turned her head away, speaking now directly to Kai again. "Go on, dear, he's in there. Just resting." She all but patted Kai on the head and drifted off in the direction of the kitchen, humming to herself.

Kai's petite frame filled the doorway as she entered the room. Her hair was tied up in two braids and secured with ribbons. Her T-shirt bore the logo of a Nickelodeon cartoon—*The Wild Thornberrys*, maybe? It fit her snugly, in direct contrast to a pair of enormous red cargo cords that threatened to slip off her hips.

Ed found himself fleetingly wondering where Kai shopped. Assuming she was interested in going to the prom with him, he hoped she'd have something a little more grown up to wear. *Reality, Fargo,* he reminded himself. "Hi," he offered. One moment more of silence and Kai would have wondered what was wrong. And Ed was incredibly determined that nothing actually *be* wrong. He was just a guy, asking his girlfriend to prom. Girl. Friend. Platonic. Casual. Cool. "Thanks for coming over," he choked out.

"Of course." She smiled. "We had to celebrate your emancipation."

She was so good-natured. `Christ, was that the problem? Did he need someone who was utterly unschooled in basic human niceties?`

"Okay," he agreed, "but no more cookies. I think

you may have caused serious intestinal damage with that first one."

"Liar," she teased. "I've seen you put away lots more than that."

He couldn't argue with the logic. "Yeah, true. But let's give it another day or two."

She nodded. "Fair enough. What are we going to do, then, to celebrate? You're all healed and everything. We should party." She peered at him, her face open and trusting. Ed knew she wasn't trying to manipulate him at all. She was genuinely happy to see him in recuperation mode, wanted the two of them to be friends. She was great.

"I know about a party," he said.

She giggled. "Oh, yeah? Where?"

"Huge party. King, queen, cheesy themes, lame, watered-down punch. People dressed in outfits that will cause them to cringe when they look back in their yearbooks twenty years from now."

"Now, that does sound like a party," Kai agreed. "I might even have some baby blue eye shadow." She laughed.

"That would be perfect," Ed said. "So you're game, then? You're saying that you'd still like to be my date for the prom?"

She nodded. "Definitely. Remember? You're my Clyde. We'll have fun."

He quickly crossed the room to where she stood and

hugged her tightly. "Excellent." He kissed her forehead. "That's the best news I've heard since I've recuperated."

Her embrace was so sincere that Ed all but gave into it, burying his head in her neck and taking in her clean scent. If his parents had walked in, Ed was sure they would have been relieved—finally, their son had been restored to red-blooded, daredevil, heartthrob status.

But they would have been mistaken. He was going to go to the prom with his hottie girl*friend*, simply and without complications. He was going to rent the corny tux and buy her a cheesy corsage. He was determined to enjoy himself. . . determined to suppress the nagging feeling that there was someone else he'd rather go with—as a friend or as more. Now that he'd asked and Kai had answered, Ed intended to do platonic prom the way it was supposed to be done.

With his determination firmly screwed in place, Ed figured, it couldn't be too long before his emotions fell in line as well. Right?

Scientific Fun Park

OLIVER RUBBED AT HIS EYES AND gazed back at the computer screen for what seemed like the umpteenth time. He had some of the world's most skilled hackers in his network of partners, and once again they had not let him down. His operatives had uncovered the computer report that outlined plans to procure "more" samples of Gaia's DNA. "More" meaning they—whoever "they" were—already had "some."

And he was pretty sure he knew how they had gotten it.

With a flash of anger he thought back to his interaction with Gaia near St. Vincent's. She had turned her back on him, shutting him out for what he suspected was truly once and for all. She had thought she was being secretive, but he knew. He knew she was up to something.

It was Loki who had originally given Gaia the gift of fear, some time ago. But Loki's gift had come in the form of a serum that emulated the chemical composition of fear. It had been false, smoke and mirrors, and Gaia had seen through the facade. But there must have been a new procedure—one that involved gene manipulation.

Loki had fears of his own. Namely that Gaia's genetic makeup—her unique, *invaluable* genetic makeup—had been altered irreparably.

His plants and hackers had recently discovered word on the cyberstreet of research for powerful new anti-anxietals. It couldn't be a coincidence. Just at the same time that madmen were cutting into his niece, treating her biochemical background like some kind of scientific

122

fun park. Just at the same time that the local burnouts were buzzing on a new drug called Invince.

A new drug that dulled the effects of fear.

He didn't think it was coincidence.

And he couldn't allow it to continue.

THE FIRST THING GAIA NOTICED WAS

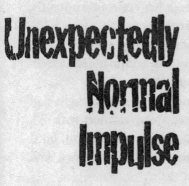

the light. The light was wrong. As in, it was dark. Growing dark. Dusk. She squinted and shook her head slowly, as if clearing out cobwebs. *Ow.* Okay, that was a bad idea. Shaking her head—however slowly—drew attention to the undeniable fact of sharp stabs of pain banging against the inside of her skull. *A headache,* she assessed. *Do I have a headache?*

She reached up to touch the spot on her forehead that seemed to be the nexus of the problem area, only to be greeted with a nagging soreness in her arm. *Okay, more than just a headache,* she realized. With great care she eased herself to a seated position, taking mental stock of every last twinge of discomfort. She was alarmed to find that there were quite a few and that they were manifest in most of her body's various extremities. *What happened?* she thought blearily.

Logic—and, of course, history—suggested that it was the `postfight hangover` she almost always experienced after a major physical exertion. It was rare for her to be so completely wiped as not to remember the fight itself, but she supposed it wasn't beyond the realm of possibility. Given the throbbing baseline of pain that thrummed through her skeleton insistently, *anything* was possible. More than possible. Likely.

She glanced around. Indeed, the light was wrong. It was nighttime. *Think, Gaia,* she commanded herself. *What's the last thing you remember?*

The last thing she remembered was daylight and Ed's hospital room. Having a conversation with Ed. Wishing him well with Kai. *Crying,* she thought, filled with contempt and self-loathing at the memory. And then. . .

Walking home. . . and seeing the boys. Three of them. They had been breaking into a house. And in a moment of what was either supreme bravery or the most inane act of foolishness in which she had ever engaged, intercepting them.

Gaia had always suspected that she was at heart a coward. People mistook her willingness to go to bat as bravery, but she knew, intrinsically, that the opposite of brave was not fearless. Fearlessness allowed her the luxury of avoiding bravery; to her, bravery meant putting aside fear and leaping into the fray. Through her fearlessness Gaia actually managed to avoid actively choosing bravery. It was almost ironic.

Today, not once but twice, Gaia had managed to be brave. Either that or deeply stupid. Possibly both. She had deliberately thrown herself into conflict on two separate occasions this afternoon. Despite being terrified at the moment of intervention.

Only now it was this evening. She took a deep breath and found that when she inhaled, even her ribs hurt. Fabulous. Now that the details of the fight were flooding back to her, she peered more closely up and down the street.

She was sitting in the *gutter*.

Literally, the gutter. Her pants were torn at the knee, and the skin visible through the frayed cloth glistened wetly with sticky blood. Her palms were caked with dirt. Tangled snarls of hair curled around her face where they'd fallen loose from her ponytail.

She'd been passed out in the *gutter*, for chrissake. Like some crack addict who didn't even know what day it was. Was *that* bravery?

Gaia shivered. She looked at her watch and saw that it was later than she'd even first thought. She'd been out cold for at least an hour. An hour that she'd been lying in the gutter, helpless, practically begging to be jumped, mugged, raped, dismembered. . . . She hugged her arms to her chest, lost in thought.

She was going to have to find a balance. She was relieved, on a certain level, to discover that even in the face of true terror, she was capable of bravery and low-level heroism. The fact that she was able to rationalize through the fear and kick ass was not insignificant. But she would be putting herself in danger, time and again, if she didn't learn to manage the exertion, to get herself to safety. Teenage girls couldn't go passing out in the gutters of New York, she knew. This was a fundamental truism.

She saw a dark spot hit the pavement in front of her before she realized she was crying. She pressed her palms into her eye sockets and willed herself to stop. This was, what, the second? third? crying fit today. That she even had to think back and count was a serious problem.

She rummaged through her messenger bag in search of a tissue, knowing it was a futile effort. She wasn't a portable-pack-of-Kleenex type of girl—which was funny since lately she *was* the prone-to-random-fits-of-crying type of girl. Her fingers brushed against her cell phone, buried deep within the recesses of the bag, and she paused.

Liz. She wasn't totally sure whether or not she could or should give Liz a call. True, Liz had been totally normal with her this afternoon at school, so she was *probably* over Gaia's weird behavior at her father's party. But *probably* still left room for self-doubt, which Gaia seemed to have in spades these days. Still, she wasn't ready to go back to the boarding-house, that was for sure. So she wouldn't even call Liz, then, she'd just go by and see. Surprise Liz.

Seeking out company—seeking out comfort when shaken or stressed—this was the normal reaction to being upset. Gaia was glad she recognized that. Suddenly stopping by Liz's apartment just to say hi seemed like a very regular-girl thing to do, and Gaia was going to act on this unexpectedly normal impulse. She didn't need to collapse in Liz's arms in disarray or even to tell Liz what she had been up to these last few fun-filled hours—though Liz might, of course, wonder why she was so banged up—but that wasn't even why she was going to head over. She just wanted to hang out for a bit, relax, unwind, and per-haps consume obscene quantities of junk food with her girlfriend. Something of the cookie-dough variety, she supposed.

And if her girlfriend's cute, wise, and attractively confident older brother happened to be home as well, Gaia was willing to endure his company. She didn't mind.

She didn't mind one bit.

far more
interested
in costly **sloppy**
electronics

Tricked-Out 007

THERESA'S WASN'T THE TYPE OF diner that did a brisk business on a weekday after school. The space was clean enough, with a bright, French door facade the staff kept propped open during all but the most humid days of summer, and the menu was typical diner fare and extensive. But it had no cachet—there was nothing to distinguish it in a neighborhood where each new restaurant that opened had a hook more opulent and unexpected than the next. It was populated but by no means bustling. Completely nondescript. Which was, of course, what made it a desirable meeting place by Oliver's standards.

He'd been waiting for Jake for nearly ten minutes now, nursing a muddy cup of coffee and tapping his fingers against the tabletop. He glanced again at his watch, displeased. Twelve minutes and counting.

Jake's tardiness was disappointing. Oliver needed the boy to be impeccably reliable, to be on the ball and ready for whatever information he had most recently uncovered. The boy was immensely eager and ready to take on even the most mundane tasks with aplomb, and as Gaia's boyfriend, he had unparalleled surveillance access, but if that wasn't the case, Oliver wasn't sure Jake would be long for this assignment.

He knew that to some, tardiness was a

129

negligible issue. But it wasn't negligible to him. He had important information to share today—he was finally ready to pass along at least the crux of his theory to the boy—and he wasn't prepared to deal with any uncertainty or dithering. With each moment that ticked by, Oliver's impatience increased.

The waitress, a chubby, weary-looking blond with a thin growth of hair above her upper lip, reached over to refill his coffee. He flattened the palm of his hand over the rim of the mug, cutting her off. It would take more than a refresh to save this cup of diesel fuel.

"Sorry I'm late," Jake gasped, sliding into the seat across the table and grinning. He didn't look especially sorry. "Subway. Freaking track fire."

Oliver didn't crack a smile. "Don't let it happen again."

Jake returned his gaze evenly.

Oliver did have to admit to himself that the boy's confidence was impressive—albeit in this case foolish. He paused, drawing out the importance of the information he had to offer. "Gaia was in a fight this afternoon."

Jake's eyes widened, but he certainly wasn't hysterical. This was Gaia, after all. Half the reason he'd even fallen for her was because of how ridiculously physically capable she was. Hardly a day went by that she *didn't* kick ass. "Yeah? So? Gaia fights all the time. What was so special about this one?"

"She passed out afterward."

This, too, came as no surprise to Jake and wasn't a cause for concern. He had seen her pass out several times, and she always came out of it quickly enough. It was the price she paid for her superhuman strength, he knew. "Did something else happen?" he asked, a slight tinge of impatience creeping into his voice.

Oliver cleared his throat, unimpressed with Jake's challenging tone. "She passed out afterward," he continued, "and spent the better part of two hours in a gutter, utterly vulnerable."

That got Jake's attention. "Two *hours*? And you didn't help her?" he demanded, eyes narrowing.

Oliver shook his head shortly. "She didn't require any help. She was on a residential side street and was left to herself. Had I intervened, she would have, of course, been tipped off to our surveillance. This is not what we want. Rest assured, though, that had she been in danger, she would have been well protected."

Jake nodded. He might be cocky, but he was also bright enough to know that Oliver meant what he said. If he said he'd have jumped in to help Gaia if necessary, then Jake knew that to be true. So he wasn't really sure what the issue was. "So what now?" he asked, toying with a sugar packet.

"You've been keeping a close eye on Gaia? On her habits, her friends, her moods, et cetera? Correct?"

"Yes, correct," Jake confirmed quickly.

"And Gaia has been more emotional than usual of late, correct?"

"Also true," Jake said, nodding. "What do you think it is?"

Oliver inhaled deeply. He seemed to be considering how much to say to Jake. "My boy," he began slowly, ceremoniously, "as Gaia's boyfriend, you've no doubt noticed that she is, as a rule, exceptionally brave. Always jumping into the fray, always seeking out trouble, looking to help out those weaker than herself."

"Yeah, that's Gaia." Jake grinned.

"What you may not have realized is that Gaia's take-no-prisoners attitude is more than just a personality trait."

Jake squirmed in his chair, his face a wash of confusion. "What are you saying?"

"It's possible," Oliver said, hedging slightly, running an index finger along the rim of his coffee mug. "It's possible that there is a genetic component to her personality—you know, in much the same way that, say, a genius has a different genetic code than a person of average or even above-average intelligence."

Awareness dawned on Jake. "And you think someone is after her to try to understand this genetic pattern."

Oliver nodded shortly. "Indeed. But more than that," he continued, "I think that of late, her genetic code has been tampered with. I think the behavior Gaia has demonstrated that has seemed so out of character is the result of a genetic modification. We're going to get to the bottom of it," Oliver said, his voice a study in self-assurance.

"God, that's crazy. How can you be so sure it's genetic modification?" Jake asked, not impudently. One of the boy's more positive qualities was that he was able to act unfazed even when presented with highly unusual information.

"For the same reason that you've suspected something is amiss. My agents have reported that she's demonstrated erratic behavior. For example, this afternoon she had a fight and expended more than the typical amount of energy diffusing the incident, which resulted in a longer time spent unconscious. Her typical postfight blackout lasts approximately thirty minutes."

"Good point," Jake said, shrugging. He didn't like the thought of Gaia lying somewhere, unconscious, for a long period. He was glad that he trusted Oliver to keep watch over her and intervene if and when necessary.

"Further, I've managed to uncover some medical documents that detail a procedure to stimulate fear through genetic manipulation. I can't imagine any scenario other than Gaia's that would call for such a procedure. Taken in conjunction with the research I've found on anti-anxietal compounds, I can't help but think that somehow Gaia—and her DNA—are involved. The question is how. Now, given all of this background—which, I should warn you, makes you highly vulnerable as a source of information—I must ask you again, and I expect you to be as honest and comprehensive as possible: Have you noticed anything at all unusual in Gaia's world of late?"

Jake paused for a moment. Oliver knew he had just passed along a lot of information to swallow. He also knew the boy had been holding back in his reports—he assumed Jake was second guessing some of the behavior patterns that seemed new and different to Gaia. But given these latest revelations, Oliver knew that Jake wouldn't dare suppress any further suspicions. Not if he was smart, and Oliver was banking on the fact that, for the most part, he was.

"She, uh, she's been acting strange," Jake admitted.

"Strange?" Oliver probed, knuckles whitening abound the handle of his coffee cup. "Strange how? I don't deal in vague terms."

Jake cleared his throat. So he was a touch nervous after all. *Good*, Oliver thought. *He should be.* "Just very. . . well, I wasn't going to say anything because it didn't, you know, *seem* like anything. But very nervous all the time. You know, her usual confidence and kick-assness, just. . . gone. A little timid."

If Oliver thought that this was important information, he wasn't letting on. But it corresponded to the fear gene theory, no question. He pressed his forefingers to his temples, looking deep in concentration, but didn't offer commentary on this piece of news. He closed his eyes briefly. "And what else?" he asked, seeming again wholly frustrated. "Anything else that can be considered new or different, Jake. No matter how trivial it may seem to you."

"Well, okay, so she's really anxious all the time, asking lots of questions and being really hesitant. So that's the one thing that seems a little off—though I'm not complaining. It's nice to have a girlfriend who isn't always looking to challenge me." He winked and laughed conspiratorially, but Oliver didn't laugh in return. "Right. And she's living at the boardinghouse, but you knew that. . . . So there are new people in the house, you know, Zan, and this other girl whose name I forget. . . but they're, like, harmless, right?"

Oliver waved impatiently, dismissing further discussion of the boardinghouse. He had all of the background information on the boardinghouse that he needed. Zan was strung out, a drug addict, and basically a waste of Oliver's time. The most she'd been helpful for was identifying Invince for what it was. . . and now that they had that information, they had little use for her. Despite her insipid crush on Jake. Or any other teenage boy that breathed. And the other girl, Alexa, was a ball of nerves who kept mostly to herself.

"And I guess she's been doing more girlie things. Like, I see her talking to the girls in school, the ones who used to hang out with Tatiana—the cool girls. Suddenly Gaia cares about them. She used to *hate* them, but now she wants to pass notes with them in class and stuff. And the Rodkes."

Oliver sat up straighter in his chair. "Who?"

"The Rodkes. Liz, Skyler, Chris. You know—their father owns that big pharm—" Jake stopped himself.

"What? Finish that thought," Oliver demanded with urgency.

"I'm embarrassed that I didn't put this together earlier. But the Rodkes own that big pharmaceutical company. I guess they just moved to New York or something, and they're new to the Village School. Well, Liz and Chris are at VHS. And Skyler is at Columbia. And Gaia's been hanging out with Liz a lot—a lot for Gaia, anyway, which means, you know, that she's been hanging out with another girl at all. But they went to some big thing the other night, a black-tie party that Liz's father was throwing. Gaia went with Liz. Which is unusual enough in and of itself—Gaia got dressed up. Gaia got dressed up and went to a *party*. I mean, when was the last time *that* happened?"

Oliver squinted, lost in concentration once more. He hadn't found any data on the Rodkes in all of his research, either. But he should have. *Sloppy*, he thought. "The Rodkes. Interesting."

"What? You think there's something there? That Gaia has these new friends? That these people came to New York? I mean, they couldn't have moved to New York just to get close to Gaia, could they?"

Oliver leveled Jake with a steely glare. "When will you learn, boy, that things are always more complicated than they appear to be?"

"But Liz? I mean, she's just this random trendoid who thinks she's the intelligent person's answer to Paris Hilton. But she's just a kid. Harmless. Wearing leather is probably as subversive as she gets."

"Well, Jake, I'm sorry if you can't see a threat in this situation, but thankfully, your input is not the final say in the matter. The fact is that Gaia is in danger—*grave* danger—and if the Rodkes are a new influence in her life, then the Rodkes themselves are subject to our suspicion. You should watch them."

"Do I get toys?" Jake asked eagerly. Alarmingly, he seemed far more interested in costly electronics than in the serious information that Oliver was imparting.

"None necessary," Oliver replied with finality.

"Your cell phone will be sufficient for your purposes for the time being."

Jake nodded agreeably, but there was an "aw, shucks" quality to his response. It was obvious enough that he was eager to go the full-on, tricked-out 007 route. Oliver leaned forward in his seat as though divulging a great secret.

"Trust me, Jake. Right now, keeping tabs on the Rodkes is the most important task at hand."

Jake shrugged. "Yeah, sure. I'll stop by the apartment. Find some reason. Check it all out and report back."

"Now that," Oliver said, seeming finally at least somewhat satisfied, "would be a fine plan."

Those who know me understand my limitations.

I have no tolerance for incompetence. In my line of work, one is only as strong as one's weakest moment, one's team as strong as one's weakest link. I have no time for simple-minded mistakes, and I am not interested in breaking in neophytes.

I have no tolerance for arrogance—other than my own, of course, well warranted as it is. I've yet to meet the master who cows me, and until I do, it must be understood and acknowledged that *I* am the master, that my rules, my quirks, and even my own limitations must be respected.

Jake may well be competent, but his sheer hubris may be his undoing. Unless he proves himself a worthy ally in the very near future, he is of no use to me. This reconnaissance job at the Rodkes' shall be his final test. Basic, to be sure, and boring, but the boy needs to learn his place. Right now he is at the bottom of the pecking order. He must work his way up. We all did, at one time or another, and the sacrifices that we made were significant.

Foolish Jake—he is wholly unaware of the extent of my knowledge. While the Rodkes themselves may still be an unknown quantity, Jake doesn't realize that I've done more digging. My research on the fearless gene, my relative success in manipulating it, has piqued the interest of some key players. My top hackers have uncovered files, leaving me no room for doubt. Those who have learned of my work are attempting to appropriate it for their own purposes. Someone intends to replicate my niece's DNA. And before long, I will know my adversary's name, Rodke or other.

As I've always known, fear-lessness is the ultimate anti-anxietal. But whereas I wanted to harness the power of the gene sup-pression to create the prototype for a fierce, unstoppable killing machine, the drug companies now wish to cash in on our Prozac nation's desire to numb every last emotion. Fearlessness would be the new Xanax, the new yoga. A new chance for people to disconnect completely, to relax themselves to the point of automation.

I won't have it.

Clearly those behind the new drug research are the same fiends who are after my niece. I won't let them come near her.

I have the files but not the sources. But it is only a matter of time. . . . And I have plenty of time. Gaia, after all, is my priority.

I'd like to protect her, to be sure, but the truth is that Gaia is mine. She is born of my own DNA if not my own flesh and blood, and I alone shall hold the secrets to her biochemical composition.

I alone shall explore these secrets, manipulate these secrets. . . .

Benefit from these secrets.

From: srodke121@columbia.edu
To: gaia13@alloymail.com
Re: What's up with you?

Hey, G.—

I hope you don't mind that I got your e-mail
address from Liz, and maybe it's none of my business, but you seemed kinda upset before and I
wanted to check in and see if everything was okay.
If I'm totally out of line, just ignore this
e-mail, and the next time we see each other, we
can awkwardly pretend it never happened.

We missed you at ABC Carpet. I bet you've got
cool taste in ottomans.

                                          —S.

frivolous,
teenage fun—
the kind she
was in
dire
need of

gaia
the
lonely
street
fighter

SKYLER WAS STANDING ON THE BALCONY

just off the penthouse dining room, appreciating the spectacular skyline that never failed to **Insufficient** entertain. At this hour the lights from individual apartment buildings glittered incessantly, and in the background Skyler could make out the Empire State Building. He didn't usually know what the colors meant on a given night unless, as on Christmas or St. Patrick's Day, they were particularly obvious, but the aura was hypnotic nonetheless. He liked to lose himself, gazing out the window, when he had something on his mind.

Lately he had a lot of things on his mind.

He heard the screen door slip open, breaking him from his reverie, and turned to see his father appear behind him.

"I'm glad you're home," Dr. Rodke said.

"Well, Liz and I got done shopping early. Anyway, you asked me here," he pointed out by way of response. "What's up?" For Dr. Rodke to invite Skyler home—and company dinners were the obvious exception—something had to be up.

Dr. Rodke gestured to Skyler, inviting him back inside off the balcony to sit down on the large sectional couch. He leaned in conspiratorially, dropping his voice. Liz, Chris, and Mrs. Rodke were all home, and the two had to be discreet. "The sample that was gathered was `insufficient`," his father said simply.

Skyler's brow furrowed inquisitively. "'Insufficient'? Meaning what? We didn't have enough of it? There was something wrong with it? Someone tampered with it accidentally? Or on *purpose*?" His pulse quickened at the thought that someone was out to sabotage their project.

His father waved his hand in quick dismissal. "I don't actually think there was any foul play involved. It's hard to say what exactly was wrong, given that it was a sizable sample. But we'll need another, and sooner rather than later. We need to perfect the compound before too much time has passed. Now that the drug has leaked onto the street in primitive form, the police are involved. They're starting to ask questions." He cleared his throat. "They were talking to Liz."

"Liz doesn't know anything," Skyler interjected. `His sister's naïveté was one thing they could count on, thankfully.`

"True enough. But for how long?" his father replied. "We can't run the risk of exposure, especially not after we've come so far."

Skyler nodded. His eyes landed on a family portrait perched on a side shelf. The three children and their parents beamed out happily. The perfect family. Skyler couldn't remember the last time he'd felt so carefree. He was glad that Liz was unencumbered by the family business. He hoped she would stay that way. "I can handle it," he assured his father solemnly.

"I know you can, son," Dr. Rodke agreed, placing a firm hand on Skyler's back. "I've no doubt. That's why I asked you to take care of it.

"Tonight."

GAIA DEPRESSED THE DOORBELL OF

the Rodkes' apartment and stepped back, running her fingers through her hair nervously. Now that she was standing here, just before their door, dropping in unexpectedly on her friend, this normal-girl business seemed shakier. Some people didn't like surprises, and Gaia didn't **A Fresh Attack of Insecurity** know Liz well enough to know her stance on the subject. Her self-esteem, never a strong point even when she'd been fearless, had definitely left the building a long time ago. No forwarding address. She tugged at her shirt nervously.

The door swung open, but instead of Liz, Gaia was

greeted with the sight of the slightly less feminine Chris Rodke. She smiled uneasily at him. From the little that she knew of Chris, Gaia thought he was funny and down-to-earth. The bulk of his opinion of her—assuming, of course, that he had even bothered to form one—had probably been solidified the day they'd sat together on the steps across from the school building. And since she'd been a mass of confusion that day, he probably wasn't all that impressed by her. Speaking of misplaced self-esteem. . .

But Chris only smiled warmly at her. "Gaia. You seem, uh. . ." He paused, considering his next words carefully, and Gaia was reminded that she probably looked like a street urchin. After all, she hadn't cleaned up from her little gutter coma. The blood crusted under her fingernails was a particularly classy touch, she knew.

"I fell," she explained quickly. It wasn't exactly a lie. "I tripped like a total klutz right off the curb and wiped out. I haven't had a chance to go home and change. I guess I look like something that just crawled out of the sewer, huh?"

"Well," Chris hedged, obviously relieved to be off the hook in terms of assessing her looks for himself, "I don't know if I'd go that far. But if it came down to you and the curb, I'd say the curb definitely won." He stepped back to allow her entrance.

"Yeah, I'm thinking of filing charges," she joked,

marveling as the words slid off her tongue that she had even managed to string them together in the first place. Witty banter was really not her thing.

Chris frowned. "Was Liz expecting you?"

"Oh, no. I actually tripped just around the corner and figured as long as I was in the neighborhood. . ." Gaia trailed off, feeling a fresh attack of insecurity. Of *course* Liz wasn't home. Liz had way better things to do than sit around hoping that Gaia the Lonely Street Fighter might stop by. She was out doing something interesting, fun, involved. . . . Liz was cool, and not in the typical, knows-what-kind-of-boots-to-wear sense of the word (though she *did*, of course, know what kind of boots to wear. Which made her all the cooler). Liz was definitely out at a play reading, or a knitting class, or an art gallery. Gaia, on the other hand, was completely not cool. . . and the fact that she thought Liz might have been just hanging around was only further evidence of the fact.

"Yeah, she actually went out with our mom. Something about a shoe-based reward, you know, for the furniture run. But I guess they should be back soon. Do you want to wait for her here? I was just watching TV."

Gaia toyed with the zipper on her sweatshirt. She *did* kind of want to hang out for a while, but she didn't want to impose on Chris since he was so clearly just being polite.

"Honestly. It's no big," he pressed, as if reading her mind. "That is, if you swear not to tell anyone that we watched *Entertainment Tonight*."

Gaia giggled almost involuntarily. Bad television with Chris actually sounded like a lot of fun. Frivolous, teenage fun—the kind she was in dire need of. "You are not!"

He shrugged. "I'm a sucker for reality TV. What can I say?"

"Hey, Chris, who was at the—?" Gaia heard a familiar voice enter the living room from the adjoining kitchen and looked up to see Skyler. She flushed, her second involuntary gesture in as many minutes. "Oh, Gaia," he exclaimed, a wide smile breaking across his face. The smile turned to a look of concern as he took in her various cuts and scrapes. "What the hell happened to you?"

"Girl meets curb," Chris cut in, waving him away. "Shhh. The show's back on."

"Forget the show," Skyler insisted. "Gaia, you're really banged up."

"I'm fine, I swear," she protested. She didn't want him to think of her as some sort of victim. For that matter, she didn't want *anyone* to think of her as some sort of victim—but Skyler's opinion of her was suddenly the one that seemed most significant. And therefore most in need of protecting.

149

He crossed over to her and took her hand. Gaia's face lit up in flames—or at least it felt that way—and she rose.

"Come on," he said. "At the very least, let me get you a Band-Aid."

"Tell me what happens," she called to Chris over her shoulder as Skyler dragged her into the bathroom.

`He didn't exactly have to drag very hard, though.`

"Now again, explain to me very slowly why the bad sidewalk did this to you?" Skyler asked, seating her on the covered toilet seat and taking a wet washcloth to those wounds requiring immediate attention. "I mean, you look like you went three rounds with a concrete mixer."

Skyler's gentle touch and rapt attention made Gaia self-conscious. "Uh, yeah. Sort of. I mean, it was a big spill," she mumbled. "Really embarrassing. I'm glad there weren't any people around."

"Forget the embarrassment, Gaia," Chris said. "You look really hurt. Were you just going to pretend you were okay?"

She looked down. He reached his hand out under her chin and drew her head back up again so that she had no choice but to meet his gaze. "Gaia. You just came over here to say hi to Liz and were hoping no one would even notice that you've been sliced and diced? Why?"

She shrugged and tried to turn her head again, but Skyler held firm. "Obviously you came here because you *wanted* us to see that you'd been hurt, at least on some level. I mean, you didn't even stop at home to wash your face. So why are you pretending as if you didn't? As if you're fine?"

And for the third time that day Gaia found hot tears rushing to her eyes and spilling down the surface of her cheeks. She hated herself for it, but she was crying again. She covered her face with her hands, mortified to have Skyler see her break down this way. He was right, of course. She could have gone home to clean up, but she hadn't. She'd *chosen* to come by. It was humiliating, having this need pointed out to her. Worse than falling apart in front of Ed, worse than waking up on the street, realizing she'd been out cold and vulnerable to any New York City predator, worse than her most acute anxiety was this feeling of being revealed, so baldly, to Skyler. Now he could see her for the pathetic, fearful loser that she was.

But miraculously, Skyler didn't seem disgusted with Gaia one bit. Just the opposite, in fact. He dropped the washcloth into the sink and approached Gaia, crouching down on his knees so they were at just about the same level. He brushed her hair out of her eyes and tucked it behind her ears, dabbed at her cheeks with a tissue, and, taking her face in his strong, wide, hands, kissed her on the forehead.

Gaia froze, and Skyler tenderly folded her into his arms.

All at once Gaia felt safe and protected in a way she'd never known. It was crazy—she hardly knew Skyler and probably should have been, at the least, weirded out about the hug, but his embrace felt familiar just the same. Skyler felt like the protective older brother she'd never had, someone who would have looked out for her during her completely atypical childhood. She sighed and wrapped her arms around his waist, giving in to the sensation of being cared for.

"Now," Skyler said softly, "tell me what really happened."

Gaia gazed searchingly into his plaintive, open face and saw no reason not to be honest with Skyler. "I was in a fight," she admitted quietly. "By accident, you know."

"My God," Skyler murmured, one hand running soothingly across her back.

"It was these three guys—I mean, kids, really, and they were breaking into this house. I was going to just let it go, but I really couldn't, and then we fought, and I chased them off."

"By yourself?" he asked, smiling. "Crazy girl." It was said with affection.

"But I... well... sometimes when I fight—"

"*Sometimes*—?" Skyler cut in incredulously.

"Well, I'm sort of strong," she explained.

Skyler took hold of one arm and curled it at the elbow, mocking Gaia's bicep. "Amazon Gaia."

"So sometimes, you know, in the park or wherever, I get in fights."

"You're like Spider-Man," he teased.

"But then afterward the energy, or whatever. . . I pass out. Wherever I am. It's like I'm just spent, and I have to rest."

And there it was, in its most basic terms. The unique nature of Gaia Moore's body chemistry just out there, on the table, for a random stranger to judge, respond to, or run screaming from. Gaia didn't know why she had chosen to be so straight with Skyler. It certainly wasn't her nature to trust people. But there was something almost magnetic about him. She had come here, after all, in her most vulnerable state. Even if she told herself she had come by to see Liz, even if she truly couldn't have known that Skyler would even be at the apartment, there was a part of her that had come to the Rodkes' seeking him out. She was drawn to him and stunned by the fact that he could make her feel safe. *No one* had that capacity or had ever had that capacity, not Sam, not Ed, and certainly not her father. Only her mother had been able to create for Gaia a sense of security.

Her mother and, apparently, Skyler. He gazed at

her, head tilted, as though considering what she had told him. "I've never heard anything like that," he confessed. "You're amazing."

"Amazingly weird, you mean."

He took her hand, his eyes mirroring only `sincerity`. "Don't say that. I think it's amazing that you would even try to take on a group of boys—that it's something you do, it would seem, fairly *often*, and that you do it even knowing that it puts you at physical risk. Even knowing what your body's reaction is going to be." He coaxed her to her feet and turned her body toward the mirror so that the two of them were looking at her bruised face. He pointed to a nasty scrape on her forehead, the one she had mistaken for a headache earlier. "*That* happened because you decided that you were strong enough to take on some punks who were doing something wrong. That's amazing." He corrected himself. "*You're* amazing. Truly."

She allowed herself to be enfolded in his arms once again, taking in the solid core of him. He was hard and soft in just the right way all at once.

Skyler pulled back from her again, still serious. "You must be exhausted."

"Well, yeah."

"You don't really want to watch *Entertainment Tonight*, do you?"

"Actually—" she began.

He laughed. "Of course you don't. That brother of

mine has such a way of getting people to do the things *he* wants to do. Listen, I have to go back uptown. A friend of mine is dropping by campus to pick up some notes in an hour, and I promised I'd be there."

"It's okay," Gaia said, trying in vain to squelch the disappointment she felt that he was leaving. After all, she had originally come by to see Liz, hadn't she?

"No, you're not getting me," Skyler pressed. "Why don't you come with me?"

Gaia blinked. "Come with you back to your dorm room?"

"Well, for starters, it's actually an apartment. But it's not like that, I promise," he explained.

"No, of course not, I didn't mean to suggest. . . ," Gaia babbled, embarrassed yet again. *Duh.* Of course he wasn't trying to get her back to his dorm room to molest her. What was *wrong* with her? Some guy—practically a stranger—actually decided to take pity on her and befriend her, tried to *take care* of her, and she had to go and accuse him of some kind of perverted hidden motives? *No wonder you can't keep a friend around, Gaia*, she thought blackly. *You have serious emotional problems.*

Skyler stopped her with a hand on her shoulder. "Don't worry. I'm not offended. Believe me, I've got thicker skin than that. But you're tired, and you obviously need rest. You're not going to get it around here, that's for sure, or at that crowded boardinghouse."

"You think it will be quiet at your campus?" she asked incredulously.

Skyler chuckled. "Okay, fair enough, but it's not like *Animal House* or anything. My apartment, be it ever so humble, is in a real residential area. Just off campus—118th Street, but situated amidst the homes of real-people with real people lives. My roommate has lab tonight. You can relax on the couch. Or if you want, I'll chill out on the couch, and you can rest in my bed. No funny business, I swear. I'm like your older and much wiser brother. Your brother who has a ton of reading to do, to be perfectly honest. But like I said, my friend's coming by, and I have to meet him. And I hate to leave you like this."

I hate to leave you like this. Gaia tried to count in her mind the number of times in her life someone had actually uttered those words to her. Not Jake this morning, who had seemed perfectly content to saunter off and leave things unsettled between them, not Sam, who wanted nothing more to do with her—and who could blame him—not Ed, who was slowly but surely moving on from their romance toward a hazy new definition of friendship that neither of them seemed to understand just yet. Certainly not her father, who'd been quasi MIA in one form or another since she was twelve. And the one person who *would* have said something like that—her mother—hadn't had the chance to.

Gaia swallowed, wanting more than anything to hide away in Skyler's apartment forever. The reassurance he'd given her in just the past few moments was like a drug. She wanted more.

"But the woman who runs my boardinghouse, Suko...," she started, not really meaning it anymore.

"You can call her from my place and let her know where you are. It's not a maximum-security facility, right? I mean, you *are* allowed out every now and then?"

Gaia smiled. "Of course."

"Well, that's it, then," Skyler stated with finality. "Run a brush through your hair, splash some water on your face, and we're out of here."

If someone had asked Gaia why she felt so connected to Skyler, why she instantly rose to respond to his request, she wouldn't have been able to tell them. There was no good reason why she felt so completely mesmerized by this person whom she hardly knew. No good reason why she was following him uptown.

But nonetheless, she was.

After all the superspy dramatic crap that's taken place over the last few weeks, on the subject of Oliver I've come to one conclusion:

I have no idea what to make of him.

Just when I think I've got the guy pegged, when I'm sure I know exactly what he's all about, he goes and does or says something that gets me spinning. It's like he's a different person every time I see him. And that person—whichever person it is that he is, I mean—that person always seems to like me, to get along with me, to want me around, but there's something going on, too. A subtle difference beneath the surface. And while I wouldn't go so far as to say that I outright don't trust him, I'm starting to get why Sam and Gaia are so suspicious of him.

For example:

1. In order to win back Gaia's loyalty, he hiked off to

Siberia to rescue his twin
brother. I'd say that's pretty
impressive. A check in the pro
column. But:

2. His brother, when rescued,
   suffered a massive spaz-out
   and rejected the help of his
   twin. When your twin brother—
   who happens to be trapped in a
   Siberian prison—doesn't want
   anything to do with you, even
   if it means his own rescue,
   that's not a good sign.
3. He made another attempt to
   reconcile with his brother,
   which he hoped would, again,
   win back Gaia, who he also
   rescued from being hit by a
   car (does that count as one
   point or two?). Saving Gaia
   from death as roadkill?
   Definite good thing. But consider:
4. His continued concern for Gaia's
   well-being has evolved into a
   twenty-four-hour surveillance of
   the girl. On the one hand, I'm
   all for it. Gaia is always getting into trouble—the dangerous,

knife-fight-in-the-park kind of
trouble, I mean. So a second
pair of eyes couldn't hurt. But
there's a nagging, small voice
in my head that says maybe it's
a little creepy, too, this spying thing.

Ultimately? I believe that
Oliver is a good man who has
Gaia's welfare at heart. I mean,
why else would he waste my time
and hers with the chasing and the
pleading and the begging for forgiveness?

But *ultimately* is really just
the bottom line. It's at the bottom. At the bottom of this backpack of mine where I have a
brand-new traceless cell phone
with a digital camera built in
and a micro-mini disc recorder
that's smaller than my watch,
almost (he finally gave in on the
toys). . . all for spying on my
girlfriend.

Something about this doesn't
add up. If I asked my buddies, or
my father, or anyone whose opinion I valued, if I said to them,

"Say, you know what? I'm heading over to some classmates' house to check it out and see what, if anything, they know about my girlfriend, because someone is out to hurt or even kill her and it just may be them. What do you think of that?" I have a pretty good idea what their response would be. After they got over the whole "are you crazy?" part of it, they'd remind me that, for starters, spying is illegal. And icky. And definitely not something nice guys do to their nieces—or their girlfriends.

But I'm not going to ask them. Because there's one other fact here, at the bottom of it all:

Is Oliver crossing the line? Undoubtedly. And is he dragging me into his slightly shady world? Totally. I'm crossing over into some tabloid romance territory with this espionage thing, for sure.

But the bottom line is that somehow, I just don't mind.

From: megan21@alloymail.com
To: gaia13@alloymail.com
Re: Prom

Hey, girlfriend—

    Ran into your man downtown while we were shop-
ping and he definitely seems excited about prom.
I think you might want to reconsider doing some
dress shopping!

    But seriously, we've been talking. Don't
freak, no drama, but you seemed kind of tense
about all things Jake related today in class, and
we've all *totally* been there. We thought it might
be fun to do some shopping and female bonding.
There could be large amounts of designer coffee
drinks involved, possibly iced. What do you
think? We'll find your dream dress, and then how
could you *not* be prom bound?

    I'll bet Liz would come, too.

                    lmk,

                    meegs

From: megan21@alloymail.com

To: melanie@alloymail.com, laura@alloymail.com,
      tammiejammie@alloymail.com

Re: Gaia

Ladies—
   We're going shopping.
   Game faces, please.
                     —M.

There was no
way his
girlfriend,
the one for
whom he
was doing
all this,
was
interested
in someone
else.

green

fury

Memo

From: K
To: L
Re: Genesis

    Have ascertained—whoever is after the subject
is in search of her DNA. Looking for the secret
to fearlessness? More research needed. Suspect
they are seeking samples, i.e., hair.

    Operatives will keep watch, prevent anyone
from getting too close.

    But who is JM? Why so heavily involved? Could
be risky to bring an inexperienced operative into
the mix.

Memo

From: L
To: K
Re: Re: Genesis

Subject's DNA is to be protected at all costs.
DNA research must be prevented.

Don't concern yourself with JM. He is useful,
but an afterthought.

And he will be fully compliant.

JAKE COULD HEAR THE STRAINS OF some reality-based dreck echo from what must have been the Rodkes' television into the hallway. *American Idol*. He winced, wondering if the neighbors minded being serenaded by this shameless display of unchecked human impulse. He himself found Clay's voice to be endlessly grating. He dug into the front pocket of his jeans and flipped the tiny switch on the mini–disc recorder to on, repositioning it so that the minuscule mike was facing outward. He was as ready as he'd ever be. Besides, he reminded himself, he had faced down serious criminals in Siberia—not to mention Washington Square Park. There was no reason to feel like he couldn't handle a little recon, at his classmates' apartment, no less. No sweat. He rang the doorbell confidently.

"Are you expecting anyone?" he heard Liz call out from inside. The voice grew closer, and he knew she'd gotten up to answer the door. Before anyone in the apartment could answer, the door swung open.

Jake had to admit, Liz was hot. She had changed out of her school clothes and was lounging in striped cotton capri pants and a thin-strapped tank top. Her features didn't have the same exotic quality that Gaia's

Ominously Plausible

did, but her all-American good looks were undeniably impressive, and even now, relaxing at the end of the day, she managed to seem pulled together, fresh, and flawless.

"Hey." She smiled, seeming confused but perfectly friendly. "If you're looking for your girlfriend, she supposedly came and went already. At least that's what I'm told. She didn't bother to stick around to see me."

"Gaia was—Gaia left?" *Swift, Montone.* He hadn't known that Gaia was headed over to the Rodkes', not that she usually kept him apprised every time she left the house. But he'd almost blown a perfect cover. *Liz* didn't know that he didn't know that Gaia had come by. He readjusted quickly. "Oh, man. I was hoping to catch her. We've been missing each other all day." Before Liz could respond, he maneuvered his way past her and into the front foyer of the apartment. If she thought it was odd that he was forcing his way into her apartment, she didn't comment. She stepped aside and followed him into the living room, where Chris sat, zoned out in a pair of Columbia sweats that had seen better days. His eyes were glued to the television, and he was robotically dipping his hand into a bag of Cheetos. His fingers had turned a dusty orange.

"Forgive my brother," Liz explained, gesturing at the lump formerly known as Chris. "He's a touch too involved with the beloved flat-screen TV."

She dropped her voice to a conspiratorial whisper, adding, "Frankly, we're all a bit concerned about it."

"Please forgive my sister," Chris retorted, not missing a beat as his program faded to commercial. "She thinks I can't hear her when she stage-whispers. Of course, that's how I get all the good gossip, you know. When she's whispering on the phone with her friends."

Jake forced a smile, though he was feeling impatient and tense. "Only child. I wouldn't know."

Chris thrust the bag of Cheetos over the couch toward Jake. "Hungry?"

"Uh, no, thanks, man."

"We've got lots of other stuff in the kitchen," Liz offered. "Stuff that isn't, you know, traffic-cone colored. Or soda. Whatever."

"I'm fine," Jake said insistently. He heard an edge creep into his voice.

"Man, Liz, he doesn't want to hear about the perils of snack food. He wants to find his girlfriend. Don't you get it?"

Jake laughed. "Yeah, I guess that's true. So Gaia's already gone?" He tapped his foot against the floor, then stopped just as abruptly, realizing he was giving away his impatience. *Very, very smooth.*

"Yeah, she came by a few hours after school, looking kind of banged up. Said she had tripped and cut herself. It looked pretty bad. Anyway, we watched a little TV,"

169

Chris said. He turned back to the screen abruptly.

"She told him she was looking for me," Liz clarified. "Not that my darling brother isn't company enough on his own, of course. I think she was just stopping by to say hello. But I was out with my mom, and I guess she didn't want to wait." Now Liz, too, looked away, almost guiltily, though Jake couldn't for his life imagine what she had to feel guilty about.

Unless. . . Jake's brain whirled as if battery powered as he pieced together a puzzle of his own conception. A feeling of dread began to creep into his system. Was it possible that Gaia had come by not to see Liz, but to see *Skyler*?

Jake wasn't an especially jealous person by nature—if anything, he was used to being the focus of female jealousy—and he trusted that Gaia was committed to him, but it was impossible to deny that they had been having problems lately. Still, he couldn't believe that Gaia would be looking elsewhere—if anything, she was suddenly amazingly needy. She wouldn't be the clingy girl she'd been lately if she had already set her sights on someone else. She wouldn't be so insecure if she was ready to replace Jake.

Would she?

Gaia's erratic behavior had been getting under Jake's skin lately, yeah, but the idea that she might possibly be interested in another guy was sending stabs of green fury to his stomach. Whatever might be going wrong with their relationship lately, he still cared enough to watch her back—*literally*—to keep an eye out for her. To come all the way over to the Rodkes' place to check them out, to make sure they were on the level. There was no way his girlfriend, the one for whom he was doing all this, was interested in someone else. No way.

He hated himself for it, but he had to ask. He cleared his throat in a vain attempt at casual. "So," he began in what he hoped was a measured tone, "do you know where she went?"

Liz blinked and dove for a Cheeto. "Uh, Chris, do you?"

"No idea," Chris said, shrugging and crunching loudly on his snack. "Sorry."

Jake could barely restrain his temper, which was starting to simmer. There was no doubt in his mind that the two were being deliberately evasive. Something about their tone, their steadfast refusal to look him square in the eye, was off. "No idea at all. Huh. Well, is it possible that she went off with Skyler?" He hated to have to ask point-blank, but it didn't seem like there was any way around it.

Liz coughed. "Um, maybe," she said, sounding uncertain. Now Jake's suspicions were in full red-flag mode. Even if she *had* gone off with Skyler, that wouldn't necessarily have meant anything. But now, with the way Liz and Chris were acting, he had to assume the worst.

"Maybe? What's 'maybe'? You didn't see her leave or what?" He knew that he was being borderline aggressive and that he'd better watch it. Given that he was a guest in their home, he really couldn't afford to push it too far. "Uh, Chris? Did you see her leave?"

Chris finally turned from the TV to regard Jake steadily. "I have no idea, Jake, who she's with. I mean, I saw her leave, but she's a big girl. I didn't ask her where she was going."

"Well, have you seen Skyler today?" Jake pressed, hoping that he wasn't about to summarily wear out his welcome.

"Yes, Skyler was here earlier. Then he left. He doesn't live here, you know. I mean, he's in school." There was a definite edge creeping into Chris's tone.

"I know."

"Anyway, I have no idea if he's with Gaia or if they were together at any point of the evening. I'm not, like, my brother's keeper, you know." He flashed another irritated look Jake's way and rose, snapping off the television set. He strode off in the direction of the kitchen purposefully without another word.

Jake wasn't sure what to make of Chris's random bout of bipolar disorder. He supposed there *could* be some bad blood between the brothers, hence the "not my brother's keeper" crap. Conversely, Chris could have just been sick of the third degree. There was no way to tell. That whole exchange had definitely been bizarre. Well, that was what Oliver had asked for—a report on the bizarre. At least Jake had something bona fide to report now.

"Just ignore him," Liz said, her voice cutting into Jake's internal monologue. "He forgot to take his medication today. Besides, he gets twitchy on the subject of Skyler. The competitive brother thing." She beamed. "Somehow I miss that fun because I'm not only a girl, but the baby. Good stuff."

Jake smiled. *Bingo.* So Chris had brother issues. Interesting. "No, it's cool. It's my fault for prying. I figured he was annoyed with all my questions. But I haven't seen Gaia all day, and she and I really need to talk. We had an argument yesterday, and things are a little strained." Not that he was looking to get into it with Liz, but maybe that would help to explain his sense of urgency.

"Hey, I get it. You want to find her. No big. It's just that every now and then Chris pulls a diva trip. It's got nothing to do with you."

Jake appreciated Liz's efforts to smooth over the awkward moment, but there was something slightly off about the conversation. Liz's bright red cheeks were like a barometer of guilt. She seemed like she wasn't giving him the whole story any more than her brother had been. Jake was grateful that the conversation was being recorded for later scrutiny. He had the distinct feeling he was missing important bits of information.

"Seriously, Liz, don't worry about it," Jake said. I was just going to stop by Starbucks and get a cup of coffee, maybe read. I'll try her on her cell. But hey— do you mind if I use your bathroom quickly before I hit the road?"

"Of course not," she replied. "It's the least we can do." She pointed in the vague direction of a long hallway. "It's down there. Have a field day."

Jake grinned, the first true smile to spread across his face since he'd arrived. "Oh, I will," he said.

Pay dirt, Jake thought, making his way down the hall as slowly as he could without being conspicuous. He figured this to be his one opportunity to get the lay of the land, and he wasn't going to blow it. The corridor was very narrow but long, with elegant moldings and a polished but much-trafficked hardwood floor. The Rodkes had money, that was obvious, but if their home decor was any indication, they were fairly unpretentious. To his left Jake passed a door that was slightly ajar. Through it he could see a small sitting room decorated in soft washes of blue and beyond that a doorway and a sturdy, expensive-looking mahogany bed. Clearly the master bedroom suite. He paused, wanting more than anything to storm in and survey the scene. He remembered, though, that Liz said she'd been out with her mother and assumed that if Liz was home, then Mrs. Rodke was as well. He couldn't risk her catching him snooping. The master bedroom was a washout, then.

The next door down the hall was shut completely. Through it Jake could hear the impassioned strains of eighties melancholy alt rock. Chris's room, obviously, and it sounded like he was in it, sulking. Probably thanks to his touchy conversation with Jake. *Nice one, Montone. Great undercover technique. Way to win people over.* Another pass.

He rounded a quick corner, quickly scanning the bookshelf nestled into the turn: *Frances Hodgson Burnett: The Complete Boxed Set, Rebecca of Sunnybrook Farm, Peter Pan, Just So Stories. . .* Someone in the apartment collected classics, and from the looks of them, old ones. Jake was impressed: the books inside the dusty, crumbling covers had to be worth a fortune. He pegged Liz as the reader. Although Chris definitely had a sensitive side, if the acoustic whine was any indication.

Two more doors lay before him unexplored: one stood directly in front of him and was most probably the bathroom, if he had to guess. That left the one to his right, which was closed completely. He placed his ear to the wood: silence. Probably not a bedroom, then—and if it was a bedroom, it was empty. Maybe

Liz's, since he knew she was in the living room? He ached to open the door and decided to risk it.

Leaning forward, he grasped the doorknob firmly. He sucked in his breath and turned the knob as slowly as he could, not daring to exhale.

With a soft click, the knob yielded. *Home free,* Jake thought gleefully, pulling the door open, again painfully slowly.

Crreeeak.

Jake stiffened and leapt back from the door as quickly and silently as he could. He paused, alert. Had anyone heard that?

"Jake? Did you miss the bathroom?" he could hear Liz call to him from the living room. "If you're staring into a linen closet, the bathroom is the door straight ahead. Keep going."

He cleared his throat. "Uh, thanks! Yeah, I took a wrong turn here."

He rushed into the bathroom and closed the door forcefully behind him. `Damn. Busted! And for what? A linen closet!` Some spy. The trip hadn't been very illuminating, that was for sure.

He reached for a box of tissues and wiped one across his forehead. He hadn't realized how anxious he'd been tiptoeing down the hall. He paused to regroup quickly. He was fast losing his cool, and he couldn't let that happen.

Okay, he thought, taking stock of the situation. *I've*

pissed off two of my top suspects and almost been caught snooping through their apartment. They're probably pretty suspicious of me—Chris definitely is.

What do I have to show for my efforts?

Nothing. Nada. Zip. Zilch.

Okay, that's not quite true. I learned that Gaia stopped by, but she's not here anymore. That she may or may not have gone off with Skyler Rodke, for reasons unknown. That's got to be important—to Oliver and to me.

And Chris. Chris is jealous of Skyler. I have no idea why—since it's not like they're competing over chicks or anything like that—but it's definitely there. Some serious Cain-and-Abel shit going on.

Unless, of course, Chris just hates me. Also a possibility.

Beyond that, though, Jake wasn't even sure the little mission had been worth his while. He sighed, smoothed a thick curl off his forehead, and leaned toward the sink, preparing to splash some water on his face before he left.

As he reached for the tap, though, he caught sight of something that gave him pause.

It was a rubber band. A basic, red rubber band. The type the mailman wrapped around your snail mail once upon a time. There was nothing of note about it. Jake wouldn't have thought twice about the rubber band if it weren't for one thing:

It had golden-colored strands of hair entangled in it.

The only person who had long blond hair in the Rodke home was Liz. And Jake couldn't imagine Liz using a rubber band in her luxurious hair. Most girls—even lower-maintenance girls—wore elastics. Stuff that was made for hair and wouldn't damage it or rip half of it out at the roots every time you went to tie a ponytail. Besides, Liz's hair was shorter than Gaia's. The hairs in this rubber band were definitely `Gaia-length hairs.`

It couldn't have belonged to a girlfriend of Chris's since he didn't date girls. Jake supposed the hair could have belonged to a girl*friend* of Chris's, but somehow that explanation didn't sit right with him. And even if Mrs.—or *Mr.*—Rodke had long blond hair. . . well, they also had their own bathroom, didn't they?

It was Gaia's rubber band. It was Gaia's hair. No question about it.

Jake flashed back in his mind to the fight in the park the other night: the Droogs had ripped some of Gaia's hair straight from her scalp. His nerves began to tingle. What was going on here? Was someone after Gaia's *hair*? And why? Did this have anything to do with DNA research?

He shivered. It was a definite possibility. And suddenly all of Oliver's suppositions and theories seemed ominously plausible.

Jake knew Gaia. If she had put her hair up, she wasn't likely to take it down later in the day. She was a no-muss, no-fuss kind of girl, and if she could have gotten away with not brushing her hair ever, she most certainly would have. So not only had she stopped by, but she had stopped in the bathroom—okay, not so weird—and spontaneously taken her hair down, only to follow Skyler somewhere?

No freakin' way.

His heart pounding, Jake ran his hands under the stream of cold water, finally dousing his face with a refreshing blast of water. He buried his face in a hand towel and breezed back to the front door at near-breakneck speed.

"You found it?" Liz called to him.

"Yeah, yeah. I found it," he called back, careful not to sound as eager and out of breath as he was feeling. "I've, uh, gotta run. I'm going to try to find Gaia." He slipped through the front door, feeling ready to burst.

"Sure, tell her hi. Tell her I'm sorry I missed her," Liz replied, her voice echoing in the front hall of the apartment.

But the door swung loudly. Jake was already gone.

Memo

From: J
To: O
Re: Recon

Trip to the Rodkes' was cool. Two things:

1. Chris is deadly competitive with his
brother. Worth looking into?

Think Gaia came by looking for Liz and may have
left with the oldest brother, Skyler. Neither Liz
nor Chris could confirm—both acted nervous and
suspicious on the topic. Not sure why.

2. Found hair band in bathroom that looked
like one Gaia would use: long strands of hair
still in the band. The Droogs grabbed some of her
hair the other day. Could this be related? I'm no
scientist, but I'd guess "they" could do DNA
research with a strand of hair.

Oliver, what's going on?

Memo

From: Oliver
To: Jake
Re: Re: Recon

Excellent work, my boy. Sibling rivalries are never insignificant, and one of the first rules of espionage is: trust your instincts. If you feel someone is being cagey, he or she most likely is.

Indeed, it sounds as though someone is after Gaia's hair. Further proof of the DNA theory and most interesting. Allow me to research further. I will let you know what I discover once I've done more work.

In the meantime, Gaia is not to be informed of our suspicions. It would only make her unduly nervous. For now, consider it our little secret.

She knew how absurd it sounded: "My **abrasive** father works for the CIA" was **sartorially** like **challenged** a lie a young child would tell.

I hate to say, "I told you so."

I hate to say it, but that doesn't mean that I won't.

Gaia can go on all she wants about how her uncle wronged her relentlessly in the past, how his crimes were unforgivable, how she doesn't want him in her life any-more. That's fine. Or it's not fine, actually, given what I now know, but I'll accept it since I have to. But the truth of the matter is that *Oliver was right.* Oliver suspected that Gaia was, once again, in danger, and he put me on the case. And guess what? I found something! Circumstantial evidence, maybe, but evidence no less that is proof positive some-one *is* after Gaia. And whoever it is, they're closing in fast. So I don't want to waste time with "I told you so's," because to be honest, I'm too busy worrying about Gaia.

It's a funny thing: When I first met Gaia, she was on fire—she was full of life and energy, even if that energy was mainly negative and mainly directed at me. I loved it. I had never met another girl like her: strong, confident, aggressive, and totally unconcerned with what other people thought of her. Capable, smart, and gorgeous, too. She was completely unique.

But lately Gaia's been a different person. It's like she's had an attack of multiple personality disorder or something. She second-guesses everything I say, she hesitates before taking action, and worst of all. . . she ran from that fight in the park the other night. Gaia would *never* run from a fight. At least, old Gaia wouldn't. It's like she's lost her edge. Her fire. Her uniqueness.

Yet. . . this new Gaia *needs* me in a way that old Gaia didn't. She wants constant reassurance, just like any other girl. And more than that, she actually genuinely needs physical protection as well. Now I have a chance to

play hero, to team with the original super-agent mastermind, to
keep guard over the woman I love.
Cheesy, I know. But I love it.

I had my doubts about new
Gaia. I was afraid that her insecurities would drive us apart.
But her vulnerability may just be
what keeps us together.

Oliver was right. Someone is
after her.

I told her so.

JAKE SNAPPED HIS LAPTOP SHUT

and ran his fingers through his hair, rumpling it further than it already had been. It had been a very long day, and he had been disheartened to read Oliver's memo requesting that he keep his discovery at the Rodkes' apartment a secret from Gaia.

Sudden Surge

True, Jake hadn't been too bothered by following Gaia around and reporting back to her uncle. But the me-and-my-shadow thing was a means to an end—and now he was at the beginning of the end. He had concrete proof: something fishy was going on with the Rodkes. And given that Liz Rodke was Gaia's de facto bestest friend, that "something fishy" could escalate to "something life-threatening" downright quickly.

He didn't want to wait.

He knew what Oliver would say; in fact, Oliver *had* said it. Oliver thought they should sit tight. But Jake didn't think he could.

He was experiencing a sudden surge of protectiveness toward Gaia in her vulnerable state, and it was clouding his ability to be impartial. Seeing the hair band in the Rodkes' bathroom had awakened a primal sense of jealousy, possessiveness, and defensiveness that he wouldn't have even guessed lay within him. Whatever their agenda, the Rodkes or the people with whom they were collaborating were *not* going to get their hands on Gaia if he had anything to say about it.

Feeling certain about his responsibility toward Gaia somehow had the effect of reinstating Jake's faith in their relationship. They'd been on shaky ground lately, but his emotions were running high right now, and at this exact moment he was willing to do whatever it took to set them back on the right track and to take care of her.

Jake wasn't a fool. He knew that defying Oliver wasn't the brightest move for a sleuth in training. But for some inexplicable reason, that didn't matter to him right now. The only thing that mattered was Gaia. Reaching out to Gaia, reconnecting with Gaia.

Warning Gaia.

With a heavy sigh—keeping in mind that Oliver had outright told him not to say anything about their suspicions—Jake picked up his cordless and dialed Gaia's cell phone. He waited for Gaia to pick up.

And waited.

He wasn't deterred by the fact that she didn't answer right away, knowing that her phone could easily be buried at the bottom of her bag. But the fact that it continued to ring rather than being sent straight to voice mail was an indication that she was deliberately avoiding it. He knew Gaia wasn't nuts about advanced technology—she was practically the last girl in New York City to even get a cell phone, for chrissake—but he couldn't believe that she wasn't answering his call. Especially since she'd been so needy of his attention lately.

He hung up the cordless and tossed it aside in frustration. What was going on with Gaia, anyway?

GAIA FROWNED AT THE SCREEN OF her cell phone. She had only just rescued it from the depths of her messenger bag, in time to see that she had missed a call from Jake, probably by one ring. She bit her lip. She *really* hated people who blabbed away on the phone in public places like restaurants, et cetera, and she really didn't want to be one of those people. But still. . . she had been trying to catch up with Jake all day, and they really needed to talk. She moved to hit the redial button, but Skyler gently grabbed her wrist from across the table.

The two were sharing a small booth at Tom's

Total Relationship Meltdown

Diner. Gaia only knew the place from the Suzanne Vega song and, of course, *Seinfeld*, which, even living in the pop culture cave she lived in, was a show she'd been unable to avoid. The exterior, of course, looked just like it did on television, but the interior was far smaller, grubbier, and more bustling with activity than Jerry and crew's version ever had been. It was an established haunt for Columbia students and a proven late-night greasy spoon. Skyler and Gaia had stopped in on the way to his apartment for a quick refuel. Both were nursing cups of strong black coffee, and a half-eaten plate of cheese fries swimming in grease sat between them on the table. Normally Gaia would have devoured the fries, leaving nary a grease stain behind. But being in Skyler's presence was. . . a distrac-tion, to say the least. And so there the plate sat, virtually untouched. Right next to Gaia's hand, which Skyler was now, even still, holding firmly.

"What?" she asked uncertainly. She knew that making a phone call at the table wasn't the most polite thing a person could do, but it was par for the course in Manhattan. He couldn't really object—could he?

"Come on," Skyler said. "You're just starting to relax, right? I mean, you don't want to get on your cell phone, start chatting, get all worked up again, do you? The whole reason you came uptown with me was to get away from things for a bit until you felt calmer."

He leveled her with a gaze that at once seemed wise as well as sympathetic.

Gaia shrugged. He had a point. "True, but it's just. . ." She didn't know why, but she hesitated on the words *it's just my boyfriend.* Even though Skyler wasn't interested in her romantically, she didn't want him to know how much she wanted—*no, let's be honest, Gaia*—needed reassurance from Jake. She couldn't rationalize it, but she wanted to keep her relationship with Skyler separate from whatever else was going on.

Special.

"It's just my boyfriend," Gaia finished, trying to bolster her voice with more confidence than she actually felt. "I've been meaning to talk to him all day, and we haven't had a free minute."

Skyler gazed at Gaia. "Gaia. Do you love your boyfriend?"

Gaia flushed, color filling her cheeks instantaneously. "Yes," she said softly.

"Good, then. And I can only imagine that he loves you, too. Which is as a stable relationship should be. But a stable relationship requires trust and understanding, right?"

Gaia shrugged. She wasn't totally sure what Skyler was getting at. Trust and understanding were key to any strong relationship, sure, but what did that have to do with taking a minute to call Jake back? She didn't think a quick phone call was indicative of a total relationship meltdown—but in this case a lack of phone call, in fact, could be.

"Um, sure, yeah," she agreed halfheartedly. She didn't have *quite* the confidence to disagree with Skyler. After all, he was being awfully caring—much more caring than Jake had been after her recent attack near the boardinghouse, after all.

"Well, then," Skyler offered, "don't you think you can wait to call him back until after you've taken some time for yourself? He'll still be there in a few hours, right? And he'll probably respect your independence."

Gaia didn't really see as how waiting an hour or so to return Jake's phone call really qualified as asserting her independence, but she nodded nonetheless. She really didn't have the energy—or even the conviction, to be perfectly honest—to argue with Skyler on the matter.

A slim, wiry waitress hopped up on caffeine topped off their coffee. Gaia lifted her mug and blew on the steam that rose from within it. She sipped gingerly, wary of the heat but relishing the bitter taste as it slid down her throat.

"Gaia," Skyler began, moving on to new topics now that the matter of the phone call had been resolved, "can I ask what you were doing picking a fight? Since I know this wasn't a onetime thing, that is. I mean, why would you do that? Continuously put yourself in danger?"

Gaia tensed. At the Village School her classmates knew she was different. They knew she was `abrasive and sartorially challenged, smart but often absent, and frequently sporting multiple bruises`. They knew she preferred wash 'n' wear and wasn't openly friendly. They knew she kicked ass in karate. But only a handful were aware of what was almost a double life, of her patrols in the park and her constant vigilance, her need to be on the lookout at all times. It wasn't something she liked to draw attention to or share. High school was hard enough for those who didn't have just the right sneakers—which usually included Gaia—and she wasn't eager to go out of her way to point out her key differences from other, normal teenagers.

But Skyler seemed so genuinely concerned that Gaia felt guilty automatically deflecting his question. She didn't know if it was their age difference or just something intrinsic to his personality, but Skyler's interest in her felt unique. Not like that of Jake, who obviously viewed Gaia as a challenge—albeit one that he seemed to find attractive—or Ed, who was a glutton for punishment in the form of unrequited love. Skyler's attention felt so uncommon to Gaia that, much to her surprise, she found herself weighing the possibility of being honest with him, which was a refreshing impulse.

The truth—"My father is a CIA agent whose twin brother went rogue and killed my mother; now we're constantly on the defensive, and meanwhile, my self-proclaimed reformed uncle believes he is my sole protector"—was out of the question. But certainly there was a variation thereof that she could cobble together; not quite a lie if not the entire truth. She paused, collecting her thoughts, before proceeding with a plausible version of the facts.

"Well, to tell you the truth—and this isn't something I usually go around sharing. . ."

Skyler ran his pinched fingers and thumb across his lips in a my-lips-are-sealed gesture that was almost comical.

"Basically, my father works for the CIA."

Skyler did a spit-take with his coffee. This time Gaia had to laugh. She knew how absurd it sounded: "My father works for the CIA" was like a lie a young child would tell in the school yard in a misguided effort to impress his or her friends. Too bad it was actually her life.

"I know, I know—it sounds totally whacked out, but I swear, it's the truth," she protested. "Why would I make this stuff up?"

Skyler nodded. "Good point. I can't think of one good reason why you would. Carry on." He gestured grandly, sweeping his hand across the table, tears of laughter still gathering in the corners of his eyes.

"Anyway, because he was Joe CIA, he was obviously trained in all sorts of martial arts and stuff, and I guess he basically felt that everyone—or at least, everyone that he was close to—should be trained in that sort of stuff, too. You know, so we could protect ourselves and whatever. So for as long as I can remember, we'd practice. I'm talking hours, every day. Mostly after school, but sometimes before school, too. Really hard core, especially for such a small kid."

"I can imagine," Skyler said, his voice tinged with disbelief and admiration.

"So now, you know, I can pretty much take care of myself in a fight. So, I mean, I'm not so much *looking* for trouble, but. . . I guess, it being New York City and all, I find it pretty easily. And if I see something sketchy going down, it's really hard for me not to step in and take care of it. Just because. . . well, just because I can."

"Wow," Skyler said softly, without any trace of sarcasm. "I stand by my words in the bathroom. You really *are* amazing."

"Well," Gaia hedged, uncomfortable to be the center of his attention. "I don't know about that. I think most people, in the same situation, might behave in the exact same way. Or at least, I like to think so."

"You give the human animal far too much credit,"

Skyler said rather cynically. "But thankfully people like you balance out the equation."

"Anyway, the thing is, maybe it's a postadrenaline reaction or something, but after a big fight I'm really wiped. Sometimes I pass out, and I usually can't control it. So I try to be careful, you know, so I don't end up unconscious in the park, but you can't always help that. Like today. Waking up unconscious really freaked me out."

"I'm sure. Don't you get scared?" Skyler asked, openly curious.

Gaia laughed a short, bitter laugh. There was truth, and then there was science fiction hour. Telling Skyler about her genetic makeup was asking for more than the typical suspension of disbelief, and she'd had more than enough honesty for one afternoon. "Not usually," she said simply.

It certainly wasn't a lie.

When had he
become **bizarro**
such a
massive **world**
loser?

It's been a long time since I allowed myself to depend on anyone. A *really* long time.

Basically I've been on my own ever since my mother died. My father split pretty soon after that happened—and I *know*, he had to, but still. . . it's hard to accept. I mean, I was *twelve*, for chrissake. I was twelve and I had just lost my mother. How mature were people really expecting me to be? Even today it's hard for me to deal with the fact that my father can't really be around, but at twelve? It was a damn near impossibility.

So. No mother and no father. The few friends that I did manage to make were hunted like animals by the man who wears my father's face. Some were killed. Some were *presumed* killed, only to turn up later, unable to deal with being part of my life (what with the constant danger and all. People are so touchy). My foster parents? Oh, yeah, double agents who

again tried to have me killed.
Mind you, my foster mother
redeemed herself in the penulti-
mate hour. And what happened to
her, again. . . ? Oh, that's
right. Killed.

It's not all bad all the time.
But my best friend, Ed, has moved
on to greener pastures, to a
girlfriend—well, a girl*friend*—who
knows how to dress, how to be
social, how to have fun. . . in
other words, the opposite of me.
My new boyfriend will very
shortly be my ex-boyfriend if we
continue on our current path.
It's no secret that I'm on his
last nerve. The FOHs have no
interest in my fashion victim
bull. . . and for some reason,
this actually bothers me. I hate
to admit it, but it does. My
uncle is stalking me, determined
that I shouldn't have even a day
of believing that maybe I'm safe,
and, of course, Dad's away again,
God knows where.

If it's Tuesday, I've got no
one but myself to depend on.

So yeah, I learned to be self-sufficient, because leaning on people who aren't actually there can be pretty difficult. I had a crash course in independence, even though I never asked for it.

But Skyler Rodke is unlike anyone I've ever known. For starters, whenever he's around, the air suddenly feels charged with thousands of tiny electrons. I don't know how or why, and I do know that I might even gag myself with the cheese I am currently spouting, but it's the truth. When he walks into the room, I freeze. It's a total chemical reaction that is utterly involuntary. It isn't going away.

And what's more, I don't want it to.

Even more unbelievable is the fact that for some reason, Skyler is interested in me. Really and truly. He wants to know all about me, why I behave the way I do, and what makes me tick. He doesn't think I'm weird for being so immune to fear (well, at

least, once upon a time)—he
thinks it's *cool*. Or so he says.
And something about the way he
says it makes me want to believe
him.

I don't know why Skyler's
taken an interest in me. I don't
know what makes him different
than other people, what makes him
intrigued instead of freaked out
by me. But I like it. I like the
way he looks at me. He gets this
expression, this sort of awe and
compassion mixed with protection.
Like if I let him, he'd look out
for me. He'd let me lean on him.
If I let him.

It may be out of character,
the idea of letting someone support me.

But it's an awfully appealing
notion.

SKYLER'S APARTMENT WAS JUST OFF

Fun Broadway on 118th Street. The block was well lit but not well populated this evening. "Is it safe here at night?" Gaia asked nervously, eyeing a trail of litter that snaked from the gutter along the sidewalk. She'd had more than her share of excitement for the day.

"Are you kidding? I've got my own personal bodyguard," Skyler teased, punching Gaia's arm playfully.

Gaia laughed, but her discomfort was apparent. "Hey," Skyler said, his voice taking a somber tone. "Seriously. We're totally safe. True, the blocks that don't house dorms or university buildings look a little neglected, but there's enough security in the area to stave off an army. I mean, can you imagine the scandal if a student was injured or robbed? The university would do anything to prevent that." He wrapped an arm around her soothingly and gave her shoulders a quick, reassuring squeeze.

Gaia found she couldn't argue with his logic. They stopped in front of a nondescript brownstone that had seen better days. Skyler fished out his keys and led the way up a staircase. He lived on the second floor of what was evidently a very dusty walk-up.

As Skyler opened the door to his apartment, Gaia was relieved to see that the unsavory atmosphere didn't extend to his living quarters. His apartment was small, but well laid out and cozy. It was immediately apparent that he was getting help from his parents in paying the rent, but then again, given that he was a college student, it only made sense.

The apartment was a U-shaped two bedroom (though, as promised, the unknown roommate was indeed nowhere to be found) with a decent-sized kitchenette and a comfortable living room. An orange plaid sofa sat along the back wall, no doubt rescued from a recent grad or flea market. The bulk of the living area was dominated by an oversized coffee table overflowing with outdated copies of *FHM* and *Maxim*. Gaia crossed over to the table and picked one up, flipping through it, amused. "'What's hot now,'" she read aloud. She tossed the magazine back onto the table. "Apparently Victoria's Secret models in various stages of undress are hot now," she reported to Skyler archly. "Who knew?"

Skyler chuckled. "What can I say? I'm a bachelor. Sue me if I like hot chicks. Besides," he defended himself, "it's my roommate's subscription."

Gaia laughed herself, pleased to find that stepping into Skyler's apartment *had* made her feel instantly relaxed. "Sure, it is," she teased. She was glad she had allowed him to persuade her to come uptown. "A bachelor, huh?" she asked, quickly stepping over to the small kitchen area. "We'll see." She grabbed at the refrigerator door handle, daring Skyler to stop her.

"Oh, hey, not the fridge—," he protested, darting

behind her and wrestling her away from the door. It swung open to reveal barren shelves but for one sad carton of leftover Chinese food sitting by itself.

"Oh, no," Gaia chided, shaking her head ruefully. "Not even milk."

"But hey—no beer. So that, at least, rescues me from being a *total* cliché, right?" Skyler pointed out.

"Yeah, I guess so." Gaia was suddenly acutely aware of the space between her and Skyler. Or rather, the distinct lack thereof. He had wrapped himself around her to pull her away from the refrigerator, but he still hadn't let go. His arms were tight around her waist, and she could feel his breath on the back of her neck. The air felt thick and close, and Gaia barely dared inhale. She wasn't quite sure what was going on. . . but whatever it was, she wasn't going to be the one to break the trance.

A shrill jingling suddenly sounded, shocking Gaia and Skyler out of the moment. Her cell phone. . . *Damn,* Gaia thought fleetingly, then paused to reflect on how unpleasant it was to be snapped back to reality. She reached into her bag—thankfully the phone was on top by now—and saw that again, it was Jake.

In a flash Skyler's arms were circling her, creating a heat and texture to the atmosphere that was indefinable but impossible to ignore. He pulled the cell phone from her hands, and she allowed him to. He turned it off and placed it on the small fold-out table. Reaching for Gaia's shoulders, he spun her around so that she faced him. They locked eyes.

"Gaia, didn't we say you were going to rest?" he asked, his voice low and hypnotic.

"Yes," she answered shortly. Her mouth felt dry. Any thoughts she'd had of Jake and wanting to speak with him were instantly banished.

"You don't mind being cut off from the world for a few hours, do you? Isn't it more fun this way?" He looked at her expectantly.

"Yeah," Gaia mumbled, exhausted and all too willing to give into Skyler's suggestions. He seemed to know what was best for her.

"Fun."

JAKE GLARED AT THE SCREEN OF HIS cell phone as if it were poison. Frustrated, he thrust it back into his pocket and shivered. The produce section at Citarella was packed bumper-to-bumper with shoppers, which was unexpected at this late hour. He was picking up a few items as a favor to

New Depths of Pathetic

his father. He wasn't much in the mood for shopping, but it was better than sitting around his apartment, stewing about Gaia.

Or so he'd thought.

As it turned out, leaving his apartment hadn't had the desired effect of causing him to *stop* thinking about Gaia, and so, after much grappling with the logical side of his brain (which, logically enough, told him that Gaia would call him back once she got the message), he decided to try her again. This wasn't standard Jake Montone behavior. He couldn't remember the last time he'd had to call a girl more than once, and frankly, he wasn't pleased with this new development. That was the problem with going after challenging girls—they posed all of these, uh. . . *challenges*. He stared hard at a mountain of papayas that were advertised as on special before realizing that he was fixated and backing away.

Jeez, when had he become such a massive *loser*? Jake Montone *never* chased women or allowed women to give him the runaround. He was plumbing new depths of pathetic here.

It was Gaia, he realized. When he'd arrived at VHS, he could have had his pick of any girl he wanted: the hottest, the most popular, the nicest. And he had picked Gaia, despite the fact that she wasn't necessarily any one of the above, specifically. She was beautiful, sure, and she could wipe the mat with any guy twice her size, but she wasn't even typical in any of the various superlatives of the high school scene. She was unique, and she didn't even give a shit. It had driven Jake crazy.

Now it was making him *insane*. He shook his head, willing himself away from a sign that read, Bananas—$.69/lb. *I'm losing it,* he thought. *Truly losing it.*

"Excuse you," a voice off to his right said, decidedly irritated. He wasn't sure why the voice was talking to him or why it sounded so pissy, but when he turned to face it, he realized that the reason the voice was annoyed with him was because he was basically standing on top of the voice's owner. It was Tammie Deegan, brandishing a package of semi-fresh sushi like a weapon. "Oh God, sorry. I don't know where my head is," he apologized.

"Jake," Tammie cooed, her voice instantly softening. "No big. I was just, like, whoa—what's up?" She giggled.

He gestured toward her food. "Dinner?"

She frowned. "Yeah, the housekeeper made pasta, and I was like, hello, carbs much?"

Jake thought about pointing out the carbohydrate content of sushi rice or, for that matter, her negligible body fat percentage, then decided to leave well enough alone. "Yeah," he agreed tonelessly.

Tammie picked up on the edge in his voice. "What's wrong?" she asked.

Jake sighed. "Nothing, really. I've just been trying to get in touch with Gaia all day." He tried to keep his voice casual. The last thing he needed was for Tammie and her cronies to get involved with his relationship drama BS.

"Hmmm. I haven't seen her since school. I know." She brightened. "Have you checked at the Rodkes'?"

Jake glared, trying to temper his flaring emotions. "I stopped by there earlier, but she wasn't around." He hitched up his jeans, preparing to leave. He definitely wasn't interested in discussing the matter with Tammie much longer. "No big deal. I'm sure I'll talk to her later."

"Yeah, well, when you see her, tell her to e-mail me," Tammie said, surprising Jake entirely. "She seemed, uh, pretty stressed out in school today, and I sort of, like, felt bad for her."

Now Jake was thoroughly bewildered. When had he stumbled into bizarro world? He was getting the runaround from his girl-friend, but the FOHs were concerned about her? Where *was* he, anyway?

And how the hell was he going to get out?

GAIA STRETCHED LUXURIOUSLY ACROSS

Hiding Out

the orange couch, kicking off her scuffed sneakers and putting her feet up. Despite its appearance, the couch really was incredibly comfortable. All those years of being passed from dorm to dorm must have broken in the cushions. She felt like she could sleep here for hours. Skyler had suggested that they watch a DVD— *The Godfather*, further cementing her idea of him as the prototypical college male—but she didn't think she could keep her eyes open for a minute longer. There was only so much that the powers of Al Pacino could do. She was exhausted; there was no getting around it.

Skyler was right: turning off her cell phone had been a fantastic idea, as was the idea of hiding out uptown. Gaia was loose and relaxed in a way she didn't think she'd known before. She loved it. She wished she could stay here forever, avoiding the social anxieties of school, the quiet, self-contained suffocation of the boardinghouse, the constant threat of her uncle hovering overhead. Hiding out was a vast improvement over the typical crap she dealt with. Even if it was only a temporary fix—she'd take it.

She could hear Skyler sitting at his desk, typing away at his shiny laptop. He'd said he wanted to check his e-mail quickly, but now he was missing the beginning of the movie. Not that it mattered much. Gaia giggled. Worrying that Skyler was missing the beginning of the movie was silly. Considering that she herself was lying across the couch with her eyes closed.

Suddenly she felt a hand on her head. "Gaia, are you sleeping?" Skyler asked in a hushed voice. He ran his palm over her scalp, tickling her.

"Mmmm. . . not yet," she responded, allowing herself to drift off. "Did you have lots of e-mail?"

"Some," Skyler whispered. "You know, notes from classes and stuff." He ran his fingers through her hair softly, soothingly. "You can sleep. Sleep as long as you want to."

Memo

From: S
To: T
Re: DNA

New hair sample will be obtained this evening, without fail and without detection. Prepare the labs: sample will be deposited tomorrow morning.

When faced with a daunting problem, I find it most helpful to examine the facts objectively. So let's do that, shall we? Here are the facts, as I know them:

1. Gaia has allowed herself to endure genetic manipulation that has rendered her pervious to the sensation of fear. Having no prior experience with the emotion, she is hypersensitive to fear and therefore vulnerable both physically and mentally.
2. The same people who have rendered my niece fearful are looking to replicate her fear gene suppressant for their own purposes, in the form of antianxietal pharmacology.
3. A beta format of the drug has made its way to the street and is being appropriated by thugs for their own petty crimes and cheap thrills.
4. Whoever is after Gaia—and therefore after the drug—is

DELIVER

probably connected to the
Rodkes. Dr. Rodke is, it must
be noted, a scientist of
extreme repute and well versed
in the areas of biochemistry
and genetic composition.

The facts, such as they are,
are not subtle. If Gaia weren't
lost to me, I'd warn her. But she
wants nothing more to do with me
for now. Thus all I can do is
bide my time, maintaining my surveillance and ensuring her
safety. I may never win her trust
back, but I can't risk losing her
to the agents that threaten her
safety. Because Gaia may be lost
to me, but there's one more fact
that I am fast coming to face:
Oliver is lost to me as well.
And Loki's got plans for the
future.

here is a
sneak peek of
Fearless™ #34:
FAKE

His eyes
were like **bitch-**
a pair of **slapped**
floodlights—
bright, **by**
steady,
reality
mesmerizing.

LOKI STOOD BEFORE HIS 17TH-STORY

Pawn

window staring out at the night sky. The nearby buildings were cast in a palette of varying grays, like the set of a Japanese monster movie. Beyond them, the city's lights stretched out toward the horizon like tiny holes in the threadbare darkness.

She was out there somewhere. His Gaia. Possibly behind one of those pricks of light. Maybe even fighting for her life.

Normally he would not worry. She was strong, his girl. A modern Valkyrie. He had no doubt she could overpower or outmaneuver anything the city threw at her. But this was different. Right now she was in the hands of someone he didn't trust—someone who also realized what invaluable gems she carried in her genetic code.

He turned his back to the window and snatched his alpha-numeric pager off the rim of his slacks. He held it up, letting the city lights bounce off the sleek black display screen. Still no messages. He set the pager down on a nearby console and pulled a 50-cent piece from his left pocket. Then he turned the coin over and over in his hands, feeling the metal grow warm in his grasp.

He could send out an alert, rally all of his operatives in the search for Gaia. But that would be rash. It was quite possible one of them had turned on him, passing along vital secrets to his competitor. Ever since his return, it had been difficult to know his men's loyalties. All those

3

weeks he lay useless in a hospital bed, they had been cut off and left to fend for themselves—body parts without a brain. He could almost understand it if one of them had latched on, leech-like, to another willing leader.

Patience, he thought, as he repocketed his coin and walked over to the teak and leather bar on the opposite side of the room. He would not send out an APB. Frustrating as it was, it would be far better to wait than risk informing his nemesis of his panicked state.

Plus, he had the boy.

It was not the same. Jake Montone was no operative. He had no subtlety. And he lacked the necessary ability to surgically sever all emotional ties and simply follow orders. The boy complicated things, but he did have one advantage that a whole team of trained professionals, including Loki himself, did not have: Gaia, for some reason, trusted the boy.

And he's proving easy to mold, Loki submitted generously, filling a highball glass halfway with ice cubes and drenching them in amber-colored scotch. He is green, but enthusiastic—eager to be Gaia's knight in shining armor.

As long as he was a willing servant and Gaia let him near her, he would continue to use the boy. Jake was not much of a secret weapon in a crisis such as this. But then, given the right circumstances, even a pawn can defeat a king.

THE SCREEN FADED TO BLACK. THE

Dust Bunny From Hell

theme music swelled, filling the apartment with its mournful melody. Gaia lay across the butter-colored leather couch, her head in Skyler's lap. The turquoise and navy Columbia University blanket he had tossed over her was making her arm itch, but she didn't scratch. She could feel Skyler stretch his arms—first up, then out—but she remained immobile, her eyes transfixed to the words scrolling up the 36-inch television screen. She was motionless yet tense, like a spring-loaded trap, powerless to untangle her mind from the Godfather universe.

All those times she'd watched the movie, she'd never realized how disturbing it was. In fact, she never imagined a movie, especially one she'd seen before, could cause such seismic emotional activity. Chalk it up to another perk of the fear gene. As an added bonus, it makes movies much more exciting!

Her gut felt bunched and her heart seemed to be throbbing in pain instead of simply beating. The whole time she watched the film, an awful dread crept over. She felt vulnerable and exposed, as if a cold-blooded gunman might jump out from behind the couch at any moment.

And knowing her life, it could happen.

Skyler placed his hand on her shoulder and shook it gently. "You awake?" he asked in a murmur.

"Mm-hmm," she replied. She sat up slowly, hugging her knees to her chest.

"So, you want to watch something else?" Skyler asked, hitting the power button on the remote. The music stopped suddenly. Now all Gaia could hear was the thudding of her heartbeat and the nasal whine of her breathing.

She shook her head.

"Okay. So what do you want to do?"

What did she want to do?

The world of Mafiosos was gradually fading as her own reality took back color and form. Skyler's apartment was all foreign shadows. She could make out the familiar lump of her backpack, still streaked with mud from her tussle with the IV-heads. Her jacket lay across a nearby chair. It looked rumpled and neglected, a forlorn shape among all the blocky masculine furniture.

A siren sounded nearby, screeching louder and then dopplering away. Gaia drew her legs tighter against her chest. Her world wasn't any better than the movie one. In fact it was worse. Hers was darker, more chaotic. Existing in it made her feel worn out and defeated—bitch-slapped by reality. Right now all she wanted was to curl up and ignore everything forever.

"Gaia?" Skyler prompted.

"I think I need to go," she said, pushing off the couch and reaching down for her tennis shoes.

"What?" Skyler sat up straight, his thick brows scrolling together over his nose. "Wait a second. I thought you were staying over. What's wrong?"

Gaia felt a pang of guilt as she tied her shoes. Skyler had been so nice to take her in after the fight. It wasn't his fault she'd turned into a big, depressing lump. But she wouldn't be any fun if she stayed around. A college guy like Skyler had better things to do than babysit a scared high school girl. "I'm sorry. I just don't feel up for much," she said, rising to her feet. "Where's my phone? Can I have it back?"

He smiled crookedly. "No."

"Ha, ha. Very funny," she said weakly. "Now please. Give it here."

"Uh-uh," he settled back against the couch cushions and put his hands behind his head. "Look, you're all worked up again, I can tell. And the whole point of you coming over here tonight was to relax, right?"

"Yeah, but—"

"No. No arguments. I'm not going to let you leave until I've accomplished my mission."

Gaia stared at him. His eyes were like a pair of floodlights—bright, steady, mesmerizing. She could feel herself wilting beneath them, until finally, she sank back onto the couch beside him.

He was right. It was late. Besides, after the fight and the movie, she was too weirded out to face the city beyond the doors just yet.

"Okay," she said, kicking her shoes back off. "But I'm warning you, I'm not going to be any fun."

"Fine. No fun allowed." He sat back and crossed his arms over his chest, his face a mask of seriousness. She could tell he was trying to make her laugh, but she was way too depressed for it to work. Still, she managed a feeble smile to be polite.

"Here." He turned the TV back on and handed her the remote. "Now, I want you to know I don't do this for just anyone. Relinquishing channel surf power is about the highest honor I can give you."

"Thanks." She settled back and began pressing the channel button, assessing each image as it passed. A medical drama? No. Men in suits talking about war? No. Late night hosts joking about war? No. A live report from a 10-alarm fire in the Midwest? Cartoon characters braiding each others' intestines? No. No. No way in hell.

Gaia switched off the power, feeling more distressed than ever. Two hundred channels and all of it unsettling. Why had she never noticed how terrible TV was?

"Don't feel like watching anything?" Skyler asked. His eyes were wide and wary, as if he feared any moment she might start bouncing around his apartment like a crazed Looney Tunes character. And what made it worse was, she couldn't promise she wouldn't.

"Not really," she said, handing him back the remote. "If you don't mind, I think I'll just go lie down." She stood and stretched out her arms for effect.

Actually she wasn't necessarily sleepy, but she did feel wrung out, like a raggedy dishrag that had scrubbed too many pots. She could almost hear the commercial: Gaia Moore, human SOS pad—use her to scour scum off the city streets, then discard her into the nearest ditch!

"No problem. I'm sure you're tired." He stood and placed a steady hand on her shoulder. "You've been through a lot."

Gaia closed her throat tightly and stared down at her threadbare athletic socks. "Thanks," she mumbled, pondering the hole over her big toe. She didn't want to meet his eyes. As it was, his consoling touch had sent a fresh fountain of self-pity surging through her. Any more niceness and she'd be all blubber.

"Here," he said steering her toward the bedroom, "Let me show you the –"

"No," she interrupted, sliding out from under his hand. She didn't want him to come with her. She was too close to breaking down; too close to revealing how raw and weak she really was. She may not be fearless anymore, but she still had that loner instinct against letting people see her vulnerable. And Skyler had already seen too much.

"Don't worry. I'll be okay," she said, lifting her head but not quite meeting Skyler's gaze. "Thanks for everything. Goodnight."

She trudged around the corner to the darkened bedroom. The light from the living area revealed a king sized bed, a workout bench, and a tall oak dresser covered with gadgets and papers. Leaving her clothes on, Gaia slipped under the thick denim comforter and curled into a fetal position.

But she couldn't sleep. She couldn't relax or disconnect her mind. With nothing to see or hear, her thoughts veered inward, each one slowly deforming into a paralyzing fear. She thought of her dad, then wondered where he was, then panicked that he might be in danger. She thought of Ed, then pictured him cozy with Kai, then fell into an agonizing nostalgia for him. Dad? Ed? Sam? Jake? Everything warped grotesquely. Everything led to misery.

And amid all the disturbing thoughts was another, vague dread. It was as if she could feel the evil of the city seeping in through the cracks in the building, surrounding her, collecting under the bed like a gigantic dust bunny from Hell. Having grown up fearless, she'd never entertained childlike terrors of monsters under the bed or getting sucked down the bathtub drain. But now, with the creeping panic overtaking her mind, she could understand such fears. Lying there, curled up and alone on in a chilly bedroom, it seemed quite possible—even likely—that this amorphous wickedness could reach up from beneath the bed, encircle her with its cold, clammy arms, and pull her down, down into a choking black abyss. If she stayed still and silent, maybe it wouldn't notice her. Maybe it would just go away.

10

Gaia's hand gripped the top of the mattress; her breath coming in short, ragged gasps. How did people do this? How did they live with their fears? The real world is such a nightmare—she knew it before, but now she could feel it. Everywhere there was danger, hatred, malice. She could see why people turned to drugs and alcohol, or formed gangs and Mafias—the better to fight corruption with corruption.

But what did she have? How could she cope? Was there absolutely nothing that could give her comfort and let her sleep at night? She closed her eyes and performed a quick mental Google until she finally hit upon a face. . . the most beautiful face in the world. Her mother. That's what she wanted right now. Her mom's lilting voice and soft, cool touch. Only. . . she couldn't have that. She could never have that again.

Hot tears gathered behind her closed lids and a jagged lump rose in her throat. Just then, Gaia heard a shuffling sound and felt the bed quake slightly. A hand touched her forehead. Mom? No. It was Skyler. She felt him slide under the covers and contour his body around hers, his chest against her back, his knees folding into the angle of her legs. He was still dressed. She wondered if she should open her eyes and look at him, but she continued to feign sleep, wondering where this was leading.

Then suddenly, she felt a warm weight on her. Skyler's left arm circled around her middle, his elbow nestled in the crook between her hip and ribcage. Gaia felt strangely reassured by the gesture. It was as if his arm were mooring her down, preventing her from spiraling off into the nightmare void. Gradually, her panic subsided and her thoughts became less and less tormenting, until they finally took on the fuzzy, garbled quality of pre-sleep.

Gaia reached up and placed her right hand on Skyler's forearm, before finally drifting off.

A SMATTERING OF RAINDROPS SMEARED

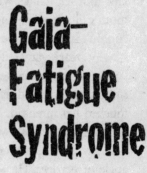

the ink on the battered computer printout in Jake's hand. Great, he thought. Just what I need.

He'd already wasted two vital hours walking Broadway and Amersterdam, checking each of the Columbia University dorms for one Skyler Rodke—rich pretty boy and possible kidnapper. Too bad he didn't hit the 114th Street student housing first. Just his luck to find the guy in the last possible place.

He headed down the block, verifying the addresses against the list in his hand. Eventually he stopped and stared at a somber red-brick building. This is the last one, he thought, crumpling up the paper and tossing it into a nearby wrought-iron trashcan. Skyler has to be here.

Skyler Rodke. Even his name sounded like a soap opera scandal waiting to happen. Jake's fingers opened and closed into fists, eager for the chance to collide with Skyler's salon-product enhanced skin and reshape his Prince William nose.

"Easy," Jake whispered to himself, digging the blunt points of his right knuckles against his left palm. He had to be cool about this. He was there as an operative, not a boyfriend. Going Jet Li on the guy would screw up the mission.

He could only hope Rodke picked a fight first.

He had this friend once, a karate buddy. The guy dropped out of classes at the dojo because he came down with some sort of chronic fatigue virus. He said it was a disease he would never get rid of. It just dawdled around in his system, waiting for his body to get the slightest bit weak. Then it would spring into action, making his joints ache and his muscles floppy, until the guy just had to go to bed for a couple of days or weeks, waiting for it to pass.

At the time Jake didn't buy it. It sounded like some cockamamie cover story. The guy was probably too lazy or chicken to put in the required effort for black-belt status and just didn't want to face the truth.

Now Jake believed him. He, too, felt like he was also carrying around a pernicious little germ that liked to kick him when he was down. He was infected with Gaia Moore. And it wasn't a one-time thing either. He was a Gaia carrier, a victim of Gaia Fatigue Syndrome.

Once Gaia had come into his life, nothing had been the same. It was as if some small scrap of her inhabited his body, set up shop, and rewrote his chemical code. His priorities did a complete Chinese fire drill, rearranging themselves into a basic, fixed list: Gaia, Gaia, eat, sleep, Gaia.

It wasn't just that he was in love with her. That was way too crude a term. This was more sweeping and uncompromising, more . . . disease like. At times he felt giddy and feverish with devotion to her. Other times he felt pulled down by her, wearied by all the turmoil in her life that was now seeping into his own.

But there was no escaping it, no purging Gaia from his system. As weird as she's been behaving lately, she was part of him now. To cut her out he'd have to destroy himself. Besides, he didn't want to be free of her. He loved the messy, aching, maddening ride that was Gaia. He'd never felt more alive in his entire life. Gaia had given him a purpose, a calling, a brand new realm to exist in. He couldn't help feeling that everything that ever happened to him had led him to this—to her.

If only something would lead him to her now.

A group of students came scurrying up the sidewalk, holding bags and jackets over their heads to protect against the rain. Jake fell into step behind them, matching their hurried pace. By now he knew the drill. He followed them up the concrete steps underneath the arched stone entrance. One of the girls at the head of the group pulled out her key card and swiped it through a black box on the exterior wall. With an irritable buzz, the front door opened and the group filed into the yellow-lighted lobby.

Jake grinned. No one gave him a passing glance as they shook water off their jackets and headed toward the elevators. He was proud he'd developed this little infiltration system on his own. It was so much easier than shouting through the outside intercom, as he'd had to do at the first couple of dorms. Plus, it made him feel like a real agent—using his wits, blending in with the crowd.

At the other side of the foyer, a man in a security guard's uniform was sitting behind a gray laminate counter. He barely glanced up as Jake approached.

"Can I help you?" the guard asked.

"Yes," Jake said, leaning against the counter. "I'm looking for a girl."

The man frowned.

Great, Jake. Brilliant opening. Now he thinks you're the world's lamest playboy. "I mean. . . I'm looking for a particular girl—a friend of mine," he tried again. He took a breath and launched into his rehearsed explanation. "You see, there's been an emergency in her family and I need to find her, but she isn't answering her cell phone. All I know is that she's out

15

with a Columbia student named Skyler Rodke. Would he happened to be listed at this dorm?"

The guard nodded slightly for a few seconds, as if he needed extra time to process the information. Then he sighed and rubbed his eyes. "Hang on. Let me check the registry."

Jake drummed his fingertips against the gray laminate as the guard sluggishly typed commands into the computer. Come on, come on. All sorts of things could be happening to Gaia. He resisted the urge to leap over the counter, shove the guard out of the way, and search the log himself.

Eventually the man pushed back his chair and turned back toward Jake. "Sorry. There's no one by that name listed."

"What?" Jake leaned forward and gaped at the monitor. "No way!"

A group of students shaking the rain off of themselves in the lobby paused in their conversation to stare at him, tipping Jake off to the fact that he was probably raising his voice. The guard held up a warning hand. "Back away from the computer, sir," he said with sudden authority.

"I'm sorry," Jake said, lowering his voice. "It's just . . . I've got to find her, and I've already tried all the other dorms. Are you sure you got the name right. Rodke? R-O-D-K-E?"

"I'm positive," the man replied. "There's no Rodke and no Skyler anything listed. Now if you'll excuse me," he added with a nod toward the exit, "I have some work to do."

Jake took a few aimless steps away from the desk, shaking his head in disbelief. This couldn't be happening. He'd tried everywhere. All that work, all that effort, and he was no closer to finding Gaia than he had been three hours ago.

What now? What the hell was he going to tell Oliver?

"Excuse me?"

Jake looked up. A pretty redhead with stick-straight Avril Lavigne hair was leaning toward him somewhat cautiously.

"I couldn't help overhearing," she said, meeting his bewildered gaze. "Are you looking for Skyler Rodke?"

"Yes!" Jake rounded on her. "Do you know him? Do you know where he is?"

The girl swayed backward slightly, her eyes widening in alarm. "I . . . I know who he is, but I don't know him. He goes to Columbia, but he lives off campus."

Off campus? The thought washed through Jake's mind, scrubbing it clear. Of course! Why hadn't he realized that before? A guy like Skyler would have his own place. He'd never stoop as low as dorm life.

"Where? Where does he live?" His restlessness was back, tightening his fists and amplifying his voice.

The girl kept her gaze on him, but turned her body away, clearly sorry she'd ever approached him. "I don't know. I've just heard he has a fancy apartment some-where. It's just the talk. You know? People talk about him."

"Right," Jake said, nodding distractedly. Then he placed his palms together in a prayer-like gesture. "Thank you! You saved me!"

"No problem," the girl muttered before hurrying back to her friends by the elevator.

Jake bounded back to the front counter. "Excuse me?" he asked the guard. "Could I borrow your white pages?"

The man gave a frustrated huff and slid the giant book toward Jake who immediately began leafing through it.

"Roddenberry . . . Roddick . . . Roditi . . ." he mumbled as his finger slid slowly down the page. "Yes! Rodke." There was a John out in Queens, a Sarah with a Chelsea exchange and then a bunch of "Rodkey" spellings. No Skyler. Not even a half-anonymous S. Rodke with a Manhattan listing. Nothing.

Jake slammed the book shut and returned it to the guard with a mumbled "thanks." Then he walked back out the front door into the rain.

Gaia was someplace close, he could feel it. But he had no idea how to get to her. He was like a rat in a maze of dead ends, and a fragrant block of cheese was sitting just beyond the walls.

Gaia please, he urged silently, straining to seek out her mind through the walls of the nearby buildings. Please just answer my messages. Call me. Before it's too late.

This probably never happens to real undercover operatives. Or at least it shouldn't—not to the good ones anyway.

I know how it's supposed to unfold. I've seen all those spy movies where the hero saves the world in thousand dollar suits. Watching them—I just knew that could be me someday, disarming the bad guys and knocking them senseless. Then carrying the hot blonde to safety only seconds before a bomb exploded in a supernova of fire and smoke.

Only lately I've had the nagging suspicion that I'm quickly becoming the Barney Fife of the undercover world. Obviously I'm not cut out for this after all, since I seem to have all the spy instincts of a garden slug.

Oliver is counting on me to find Gaia. Gaia needs me. And I'm letting them down.

I never realized just how freaking hard this spy stuff is. Where are the scared informants whispering vital information to me from out of the shadows? Where are the clues? A bookbag or scuffed tennis shoe or some other Gaia-like debris pointing the way to her hideaway? I could use a cryptic S.O.S. message on my answering machine or a taunting riddle from the baddies—anything to use as a starting place in this whole screwed up cat-and-mouse game.

The guys I watched never made mistakes. James Bond never burst into someone's lair only to find a group of women playing Mah-Jongg. "Very sorry. Pardon me. Please carry on." Eliot Ness never nabbed an innocent bystander or aimlessly wandered the city streets for hours.

Even Oliver would never be stuck in neutral like this. He'd have located Gaia in under ten minutes. I know he wants me to do it, since Gaia's still freaked into thinking he's Loki again, but obviously I don't deserve his faith in me.

So I'll make a deal with the Cosmos. Forget my earlier dreams. I don't need to be a big hero. I'll just settle for this: to locate Gaia in one piece before anything awful happens. The rest you can take from there.

As many as 1 in 3 Americans
who have HIV... don't know it.

TAKE CONTROL.
KNOW YOUR STATUS.
GET TESTED.

To learn more about HIV testing,
or get a free guide to HIV and
other sexually transmitted diseases:

www.knowhivaids.org
1-866-344-KNOW